C. S. LEWIS

THE HORSE AND HIS BOY

With Illustrations by
Pauline Baynes

PUFFIN BOOKS

Puffin Books: a Division of Penguin Books Ltd,
Harmondsworth, Middlesex, England
Penguin Books Australia Ltd, Ringwood, Victoria, Australia
Penguin Books Canada Ltd, 41 Steelcase Road West, Markham, Ontario, Canada
Penguin Books (N.Z.) Ltd, 182-190 Wairau Road, Auckland 10, New Zealand

—

First published by Geoffrey Bles 1954
Published by Puffin Books 1965
Reprinted 1966, 1967, 1968, 1970, 1971 (twice), 1972, 1973 (twice), 1974 (twice)

—

Copyright © the Estate of C. S. Lewis, 1954

—

Made and printed in Great Britain
by Cox & Wyman Ltd,
London, Reading and Fakenham
Set in Monotype Garamond

To David and
Douglas Gresham

PUFFIN BOOKS

Editor: Kaye Webb

THE HORSE AND HIS BOY

Here is another of C. S. Lewis's marvellous Narnia Chronicles. The time is the Golden Age during the reign of High King Peter, and the heroes are the Horse, Bree, and Shasta, the boy who runs away with him from the cruel country of Calormen.

Their shared adventures take them to the city of Tashbaan in disguise (Bree is disguised as a pack horse), where Shasta is mistaken for a truant prince, and on an endless ride by burning day and silvery night over the desert to Narnia, where Shasta discovers his true identity. When someone suggests that Shasta has stolen Bree, the Horse replies, 'You might as well say I stole him.'

There can be few boys who would not wish to be stolen by an animal of such resourcefulness and humour.

CONTENTS

Mt. Pire

Anvard

narrow gorge

DESERT

Rock

N
W E
S

CHAPTER I

HOW SHASTA SET OUT ON HIS TRAVELS

THIS is the story of an adventure that happened in Narnia and Calormen and the lands between, in the Golden Age when Peter was High King in Narnia and his brother and his two sisters were King and Queens under him.

In those days, far south in Calormen on a little creek of the sea, there lived a poor fisherman called Arsheesh, and with him there lived a boy who called him Father. The boy's name was Shasta. On most days Arsheesh went out in his boat to fish in the morning, and in the afternoon he harnessed his donkey to a cart and loaded the cart with fish and went a mile or so southward to the village to sell it. If it had sold well he would come home in a moderately good temper and say nothing to Shasta, but if it had sold badly he would find fault with him and perhaps beat him. There was always something to find fault with for Shasta had plenty of work to do, mending and washing the nets, cooking the supper, and cleaning the cottage in which they both lived.

Shasta was not at all interested in anything that lay south of his home because he had once or twice been to the village with Arsheesh and he knew that there was nothing very interesting there. In the village he only met other men who were just like his father – men with long, dirty robes, and wooden shoes turned up at the toe, and turbans on their heads, and beards, talking to one another very slowly about things that sounded dull. But he was very interested in everything that lay to the North because no one ever went that way and he was never allowed to go there himself. When he was sitting out of doors mending the nets, and all alone, he would often look eagerly to the North. One could see nothing but a grassy slope running up to a level ridge and beyond that the sky with perhaps a few birds in it.

Sometimes if Arsheesh was there Shasta would say, 'O my Father, what is there beyond that hill?' And then if the fisherman was in a bad temper he would box Shasta's ears and tell him to attend to his work. Or if he was in a peaceable mood he would say, 'O my son, do not allow your mind to be distracted by idle questions. For one of the poets has said, "Application to business is the root of prosperity, but those who ask questions that do not concern them are steering the ship of folly towards the rock of indigence."'

Shasta thought that beyond the hill there must be some delightful secret which his father wished to hide from him. In reality, however, the fisherman talked like this because he didn't know what lay to the North. Neither did he care. He had a very practical mind.

One day there came from the south a stranger who was unlike any man that Shasta had seen before. He rode upon a strong dappled horse with flowing mane and tail and his stirrups and bridle were inlaid with silver. The spike of a helmet projected from the middle of his silken turban and he wore a shirt of chain mail. By his side hung a curving scimitar, a round shield studded with bosses of brass hung at his back, and his right hand grasped a lance. His face was dark, but this did not surprise Shasta because all the people

of Calormen are like that; what did surprise him was the man's beard which was dyed crimson, and curled and gleaming with scented oil. But Arsheesh knew by the gold ring on the stranger's bare arm that he was a Tarkaan or great lord, and he bowed kneeling before him till his beard touched the earth and made signs to Shasta to kneel also.

The stranger demanded hospitality for the night which of course the fisherman dared not refuse. All the best they had was set before the Tarkaan for supper (and he didn't think much of it) and Shasta, as always happened when the fisherman had company, was given a hunk of bread and turned out of the cottage. On these occasions he usually slept with the donkey in its little thatched stable. But it was much too early to go to sleep yet, and Shasta, who had never learned that it is wrong to listen behind doors, sat down with his ear to a crack in the wooden wall of the cottage to hear what the grown-ups were talking about. And this is what he heard.

'And now, O my host,' said the Tarkaan, 'I have a mind to buy that boy of yours.'

'O my master,' replied the fisherman (and Shasta knew by the wheedling tone the greedy look that was probably coming into his face as he said it), 'what price could induce your servant, poor though he is, to sell into slavery his only child and his own flesh? Has not one of the poets said, "Natural affection is stronger than soup and offspring more precious than carbuncles?"'

'It is even so,' replied the guest dryly. 'But another poet has likewise said, "He who attempts to deceive the judicious is already baring his own back for the scourge." Do not load your aged mouth with falsehoods. This boy is manifestly no son of yours, for your cheek is as dark as mine but the boy is fair and white like the accursed but beautiful barbarians who inhabit the remote North.'

'How well it was said,' answered the fisherman, 'that Swords can be kept off with shields but the Eye of Wisdom pierces through every defence! Know then, O my formidable guest, that because of my extreme poverty I have never married and have no child. But in that same year in which the Tisroc (may he live for ever) began his august and beneficent reign, on a night when the moon was at her full, it pleased the gods to deprive me of my sleep. Therefore I arose from my bed in this hovel and went forth to the beach to refresh myself with looking upon the water and the moon and breathing the cool air. And presently I heard a noise as of oars coming to me across the water and then, as it were, a weak cry. And shortly after, the tide brought to the land a little boat in which there was nothing but a man lean with extreme hunger and thirst who seemed to have died but a few moments before (for he was still warm), and an empty water-skin, and a child, still living. "Doubtless," said I, "these unfortunates have escaped from the wreck of a great ship, but by the admirable designs of the gods, the elder has starved himself to keep the child alive and has perished in sight of land." Accordingly, remembering how the gods never fail to reward those who befriend the destitute, and being moved by compassion (for your servant is a man of tender heart) –'

'Leave out all these idle words in your own praise,' interrupted the Tarkaan. 'It is enough to know that you took the child – and have had ten times the worth of his daily bread out of him in labour, as anyone can see. And now tell me at once what price you put on him, for I am wearied with your loquacity.'

'You yourself have wisely said,' answered Arsheesh, 'that the boy's labour has been to me of inestimable value. This must be taken into account in fixing the price. For if I sell the boy I must undoubtedly either buy or hire another to do his work.'

'I'll give you fifteen crescents for him,' said the Tarkaan.

'Fifteen!' cried Arsheesh in a voice that was something between a whine and a scream. 'Fifteen! For the prop of my old age and the delight of my eyes! Do not mock my grey beard, Tarkaan though you be. My price is seventy.'

At this point Shasta got up and tiptoed away. He had heard all he wanted, for he had often listened when men were bargaining in the village and knew how it was done. He was quite certain that Arsheesh would sell him in the end for something much more than fifteen crescents and much less than seventy, but that he and the Tarkaan would take hours in getting to an agreement.

You must not imagine that Shasta felt at all as you and I would feel if we had just overheard our parents talking about selling us for slaves. For one thing, his life was already little better than slavery; for all he knew, the lordly stranger on the great horse might be kinder to him than Arsheesh. For another, the story about his own discovery in the boat had filled him with excitement and with a sense of relief. He had often been uneasy because, try as he might, he had never been able to love the fisherman, and he knew that a boy ought to love his father. And now, apparently, he was no relation to Arsheesh at all. That took a great weight off his mind. 'Why, I might be anyone!' he thought. 'I might be the son of a Tarkaan myself – or the son of the Tisroc (may he live for ever) – or of a god!'

He was standing out in the grassy place before the cottage while he thought these things. Twilight was coming on apace and a star or two was already out, but the remains of the sunset could still be seen in the west. Not far away the stranger's horse, loosely tied to an iron ring in the wall of the donkey's stable, was grazing. Shasta strolled over to it and patted its neck. It went on tearing up the grass and took no notice of him.

Then another thought came into Shasta's mind. 'I wonder what sort of a man that Tarkaan is,' he said out loud. 'It would be splendid if he was kind. Some of the slaves in a great lord's house have next to nothing to do. They wear lovely clothes and eat meat every day. Perhaps he'd take me to the wars and I'd save his life in a battle and then he'd set me free and adopt me as his son and give me a palace and a chariot and a suit of armour. But then he might be a horrid, cruel man. He might send me to work on the fields in chains. I wish I knew. How can I know? I bet this horse knows, if only he could tell me.'

The Horse had lifted its head. Shasta stroked its smooth-as-satin nose and said, 'I wish *you* could talk, old fellow.'

And then for a second he thought he was dreaming, for quite distinctly, though in a low voice, the Horse said, 'But I can.'

Shasta stared into its great eyes and his own grew almost as big, with astonishment.

'How ever did *you* learn to talk?' he asked.

'Hush! Not so loud,' replied the Horse. 'Where I come from, nearly all the animals talk.'

'Wherever is that?' asked Shasta.

'Narnia,' answered the Horse. 'The happy land of Narnia – Narnia of the heathery mountains and the thymy downs, Narnia of the many rivers, the plashing glens, the mossy caverns and the deep forests ringing with the hammers of the Dwarfs. Oh the sweet air of Narnia! An hour's life there is better than a thousand years in Calormen.' It ended with a whinny that sounded very like a sigh.

'How did you get here?' said Shasta.

'Kidnapped,' said the Horse. 'Or stolen, or captured – whichever you like to call it. I was only a foal at the time. My mother warned me not to range the southern slopes, into Archenland and beyond, but I wouldn't heed her. And by the Lion's Mane I have paid for my folly. All these years I have been a slave to humans, hiding my true nature and pretending to be dumb and witless like *their* horses.'

'Why didn't you tell them who you were?'

'Not such a fool, that's why. If they'd once found out I could talk they would have made a show of me at fairs and guarded me more carefully than ever. My last chance of escape would have been gone.'

'And why – ' began Shasta, but the Horse interrupted him.

'Now look,' it said, 'we mustn't waste time on idle questions. You want to know about my master the Tarkaan Anradin. Well, he's bad. Not too bad to me, for a war horse costs too much to be treated very badly. But you'd better be lying dead tonight than go to be a human slave in his house tomorrow.'

'Then I'd better run away,' said Shasta, turning very pale.

'Yes, you had,' said the Horse. 'But why not run away with me?'

'Are you going to run away too?' said Shasta.

'Yes, if you'll come with me,' answered the Horse. 'This is the chance for both of us. You see if I run away without a rider, everyone who sees me will say "Stray horse" and be after me as quick as he can. With a rider I've a chance to get through. That's where you can help me. On the other hand, you can't get very far on those two silly legs of yours (what absurd legs humans have!) without being overtaken. But on me you can outdistance any other horse in this country. That's where I can help you. By the way, I suppose you know how to ride?'

'Oh yes, of course,' said Shasta. 'At least, I've ridden the donkey.'

'Ridden the *what*?' retorted the Horse with extreme contempt. (At least, that is what he meant. Actually it came out in a sort of neigh – 'Ridden the wha-ha-ha-ha-ha.' Talking horses always become more horsy in accent when they are angry.)

'In other words,' it continued, 'you *can't* ride. That's a drawback. I'll have to teach you as we go along. If you can't ride, can you fall?'

'I suppose anyone can fall,' said Shasta.

'I mean can you fall and get up again without crying and mount again and fall again and yet not be afraid of falling?'

'I – I'll try,' said Shasta.

'Poor little beast,' said the Horse in a gentler tone. 'I forget you're only a foal. We'll make a fine rider of you in time. And now – we mustn't start until those two in the hut are asleep. Meantime we can make our plans. My Tarkaan is on his way North to the great city, to Tashbaan itself and the court of the Tisroc –'

'I say,' put in Shasta in rather a shocked voice, 'oughtn't you to say "May he live for ever?"'

'Why?' asked the Horse. 'I'm a free Narnian. And why should I talk slaves' and fools' talk? I don't want him to live for ever, and I know that he's not going to live for ever whether I want him to or not. And I can see you're from the free North too. No more of this Southern jargon between you and me! And now, back to our plans.

As I said, my human was on his way North to Tashbaan.'

'Does that mean we'd better go to the South?'

'I think not,' said the Horse. 'You see, he thinks I'm dumb and witless like his other horses. Now if I really were, the moment I got loose I'd go back home to my stable and paddock; back to his palace which is two days' journey South. That's where he'll look for me. He'd never dream of my going on North on my own. And anyway he will probably think that someone in the last village who saw him ride through has followed us to here and stolen me.'

'Oh hurrah!' said Shasta. 'Then we'll go North. I've been longing to go to the North all my life.'

'Of course you have,' said the Horse. 'That's because of the blood that's in you. I'm sure you're true Northern stock. But not too loud. I should think they'd be asleep soon now.'

'I'd better creep back and see,' suggested Shasta.

'That's a good idea,' said the Horse. 'But take care you're not caught.'

It was a good deal darker now and very silent except for the sound of the waves on the beach, which Shasta hardly noticed because he had been hearing it day and night as long as he could remember. The cottage, as he approached it, showed no light. When he listened at the front there was no noise. When he went round to the only window, he could hear, after a second or two, the familiar noise of the old fisherman's squeaky snore. It was funny to think that if all went well he would never hear it again. Holding his breath and feeling a little bit sorry, but much less sorry than he was glad, Shasta glided away over the grass and went to the donkey's stable, groped along to a place he knew where the key was hidden, opened the door and found the Horse's saddle and bridle which had been locked up there for the night. He bent forward and kissed the donkey's nose. 'I'm sorry we can't take *you*,' he said.

'There you are at last,' said the Horse when he got back to it. 'I was beginning to wonder what had become of you.'

'I was getting your things out of the stable,' replied Shasta. 'And now, can you tell me how to put them on?'

For the next few minutes Shasta was at work, very cautiously to avoid jingling, while the Horse said things like, 'Get that girth a bit tighter,' or 'You'll find a buckle lower down,' or 'You'll need to shorten those stirrups a good bit.' When all was finished it said:

'Now; we've got to have reins for the look of the thing, but you won't be using them. Tie them to the saddle-bow: very slack so that I can do what I like with my head. And, remember – you are not to touch them.'

'What are they for, then?' asked Shasta.

'Ordinarily they are for directing me,' replied the Horse. 'But as I intend to do all the directing on this journey, you'll please keep your hands to yourself. And there's another thing. I'm not going to have you grabbing my mane.'

'But I say,' pleaded Shasta. 'If I'm not to hold on by the reins or by your mane, what *am* I to hold on by?'

'You hold on with your knees,' said the Horse. 'That's the secret of good riding. Grip my body between your knees as hard as you like; sit straight up, straight as a poker; keep your elbows in. And by the way, what did you do with the spurs?'

'Put them on my heels, of course,' said Shasta. 'I do know that much.'

'Then you can take them off and put them in the saddle-bag. We may be able to sell them when we get to Tashbaan. Ready? And now I think you can get up.'

'Ooh! You're a dreadful height,' gasped Shasta after his first, and unsuccessful, attempt.

'I'm a horse, that's all,' was the reply. 'Anyone would think I was a haystack from the way you're trying to climb up me! There, that's better. Now sit *up* and remember what I told you about your knees. Funny to think of me who has led cavalry charges and won races having a potato-sack like you in the saddle! However, off we go.' It chuckled, not unkindly.

And it certainly began their night journey with great caution. First of all it went just south of the fisherman's cottage to the little river which there ran into the sea, and took care to leave in the mud some very plain hoof-marks pointing South. But as soon as they were in the middle of the ford it turned upstream and waded till they were about a hundred yards farther inland than the cottage. Then it selected a nice gravelly bit of bank which would take no footprints and came out on the Northern side. Then, still at a walking pace, it went Northward till the cottage, the one tree, the donkey's stable, and the creek – everything, in fact, that Shasta had ever known – had sunk out of sight in the grey summer-night darkness. They had been going uphill and now were at the top of the ridge – that ridge which had always been the boundary of Shasta's known world. He could not see what was ahead except that it was all open and grassy. It looked endless: wild and lonely and free.

'I say!' observed the Horse. 'What a place for a gallop, eh?'

'Oh don't let's,' said Shasta. 'Not yet. I don't know how to – please, Horse. I don't know your name.'

'Breehy-hinny-brinny-hoohy-hah,' said the Horse.

'I'll never be able to say that,' said Shasta. 'Can I call you Bree?'

'Well, if it's the best you can do, I suppose you must,' said the Horse. 'And what shall I call you?'

'I'm called Shasta.'

'H'm,' said Bree. 'Well, now, there's a name that's *really* hard to pronounce. But now about this gallop. It's a good deal easier than trotting if you only knew, because you don't have to rise and fall. Grip with your knees and keep your eyes straight ahead between my ears. Don't look at the ground. If you think you're going to fall just grip harder and sit up straighter. Ready? Now: for Narnia and the North.'

CHAPTER 2

A WAYSIDE ADVENTURE

IT was nearly noon on the following day when Shasta was wakened by something warm and soft moving over his face. He opened his eyes and found himself staring into the long face of a horse; its nose and lips were almost touching his. He remembered the exciting events of the previous night and sat up. But as he did so he groaned.

'Ow, Bree,' he gasped. 'I'm so sore. All over. I can hardly move.'

'Good morning, small one,' said Bree. 'I was afraid you might feel a bit stiff. It can't be the falls. You didn't have more than a dozen or so, and it was all lovely, soft springy turf that must have been almost a pleasure to fall on. And the only one that might have been nasty was broken by that gorse bush. No: it's the riding itself that comes hard at first. What about breakfast? I've had mine.'

'Oh bother breakfast. Bother everything,' said Shasta. 'I tell you I can't move.' But the horse nuzzled at him with its nose and pawed him gently with a hoof till he had to get up. And then he looked about him and saw where they were. Behind them lay a little copse. Before them the turf, dotted with white flowers, sloped down to the brow of a cliff. Far below them, so that the sound of the breaking waves was very faint, lay the sea. Shasta had never seen it from such a height and never seen so much of it before, nor dreamed how many colours it had. On either hand the coast stretched away, headland after headland, and at the points you could see the white foam running up the rocks but making no noise because it was so far off. There were gulls flying overhead and the heat shivered on the ground; it was a blazing day. But what Shasta chiefly noticed was the air. He couldn't think what was missing, until at last he realized that there was no smell of fish in it. For of course, neither in the cottage nor among the nets, had he ever been away from that smell in his life. And this new air was so delicious, and all his old life seemed so far away, that he forgot for a moment about his bruises and his aching muscles and said:

'I say, Bree, didn't you say something about breakfast?'

'Yes, I did,' answered Bree. 'I think you'll find something in the saddle-bags. They're over there on that tree where you hung them up last night – or early this morning, rather.'

They investigated the saddle-bags and the results were cheering – a meat pasty, only slightly stale, a lump of dried figs and another lump of green cheese, a little flask of wine, and some money; about forty crescents in all, which was more than Shasta had ever seen.

While Shasta sat down – painfully and cautiously – with his back against a tree and started on the pasty, Bree had a few more mouthfuls of grass to keep him company.

'Won't it be stealing to use the money?' asked Shasta.

'Oh,' said the Horse, looking up with its mouth full of grass, 'I never thought of that. A free horse and a talking horse mustn't steal, of course. But I think it's all right. We're prisoners and captives in enemy country. That money is booty, spoil. Besides, how are we to get any food for you without it? I suppose, like all humans, you won't eat natural food like grass and oats.'

'I can't.'

'Ever tried?'

'Yes, I have. I can't get it down at all. You couldn't either if you were me.'

'You're rum little creatures, you humans,' remarked Bree.

When Shasta had finished his breakfast (which was by far the nicest he had ever eaten), Bree said, 'I think I'll have a nice roll before we put on that saddle again.' And he proceeded to do so. 'That's good. That's very good,' he said, rubbing his back on the turf and waving all four legs in the air. 'You ought to have one too, Shasta,' he snorted. 'It's most refreshing.'

But Shasta burst out laughing and said, 'You do look funny when you're on your back!'

'I look nothing of the sort,' said Bree. But then suddenly he rolled round on his side, raised his head and looked hard at Shasta, blowing a little.

'Does it really look funny?' he asked in an anxious voice.

'Yes, it does,' replied Shasta. 'But what does it matter?'

'You don't think, do you,' said Bree, 'that it might be a thing *talking* horses never do – a silly, clownish trick I've learned from the dumb ones? It would be dreadful to find, when I get back to Narnia, that I've picked up a lot of low, bad habits. What do you think, Shasta? Honestly, now. Don't spare my feelings. Should you think the real, free horses – the talking kind – do roll?'

'How should I know? Anyway I don't think I should bother about it if I were you. We've got to get there first. Do you know the way?'

'I know my way to Tashbaan. After that comes the

desert. Oh, we'll manage the desert somehow, never fear. Why, we'll be in sight of the Northern mountains then. Think of it! To Narnia and the North! Nothing will stop us then. But I'd be glad to be past Tashbaan. You and I are safer away from cities.'

'Can't we avoid it?'

'Not without going a long way inland, and that would take us into cultivated land and main roads; and I wouldn't know the way. No, we'll just have to creep along the coast. Up here on the downs we'll meet nothing but sheep and rabbits and gulls and a few shepherds. And by the way, what about starting?'

Shasta's legs ached terribly as he saddled Bree and climbed into the saddle, but the Horse was kindly to him and went at a soft pace all afternoon. When evening twilight came they dropped by steep tracks into a valley and found a village. Before they got into it Shasta dismounted and entered it on foot to buy a loaf and some onions and radishes. The Horse trotted round by the fields in the dusk and met Shasta at the far side. This became their regular plan every second night.

These were great days for Shasta, and every day better than the last as his muscles hardened and he fell less often. Even at the end of his training Bree still said he sat like a bag of flour in the saddle. 'And even if it was safe, young 'un, I'd be ashamed to be seen with you on the main road.' But in spite of his rude words Bree was a patient teacher. No one can teach riding so well as a horse. Shasta learned to trot, to canter, to jump, and to keep his seat even when Bree pulled up suddenly or swung unexpectedly to the left or the right – which, as Bree told him, was a thing you might have to do at any moment in a battle. And then of

course Shasta begged to be told of the battles and wars in
which Bree had carried the Tarkaan. And Bree would tell
of forced marches and the fording of swift rivers, of
charges and of fierce fights between cavalry and cavalry
when the war horses fought as well as the men, being all
fierce stallions, trained to bite and kick, and to rear at the
right moment so that the horse's weight as well as the
rider's would come down on an enemy's crest in the stroke
of sword or battleaxe. But Bree did not want to talk about
the wars as often as Shasta wanted to hear about them.
'Don't speak of them, youngster,' he would say. 'They
were only the Tisroc's wars and I fought in them as a slave
and a dumb beast. Give me the Narnian wars where I shall
fight as a free Horse among my own people! Those will be
wars worth talking about. Narnia and the North! Bra-ha-
ha! Broo hoo!'

Shasta soon learned, when he heard Bree talking like
that, to prepare for a gallop.

After they had travelled on for weeks and weeks past
more bays and headlands and rivers and villages than
Shasta could remember, there came a moonlit night when
they started their journey at evening, having slept during
the day. They had left the downs behind them and were
crossing a wide plain with a forest about half a mile away
on their left. The sea, hidden by low sandhills, was about
the same distance on their right. They had jogged along for
about an hour, sometimes trotting and sometimes walking,
when Bree suddenly stopped.

'What's up?' said Shasta.

'S-s-ssh!' said Bree, craning his neck round and twitching his ears. 'Did you hear something? Listen.'

'It sounds like another horse – between us and the

wood,' said Shasta after he had listened for about a minute

'It *is* another horse,' said Bree. 'And that's what I don't like.'

'Isn't it probably just a farmer riding home late?' said Shasta with a yawn.

'Don't tell me!' said Bree. '*That*'s not a farmer's riding. Nor a farmer's horse either. Can't you tell by the sound? That's quality, that horse is. And it's being ridden by a real horseman. I tell you what it is, Shasta. There's a Tarkaan under the edge of that wood. Not on his war horse – it's too light for that. On a fine blood mare, I should say.'

'Well, it's stopped now, whatever it is,' said Shasta.

'You're right,' said Bree. 'And why should he stop just when we do? Shasta, my boy, I do believe there's someone shadowing us at last.'

'What shall we do?' said Shasta in a lower whisper than before. 'Do you think he can see us as well as hear us?'

'Not in this light so long as we stay quite still,' answered Bree. 'But look! There's a cloud coming up. I'll wait till that gets over the moon. Then we'll get off to our right as quietly as we can, down to the shore. We can hide among the sandhills if the worst comes to the worst.'

They waited till the cloud covered the moon and then, first at a walking pace and afterwards at a gentle trot, made for the shore.

The cloud was bigger and thicker than it had looked at first and soon the night grew very dark. Just as Shasta was saying to himself, 'We must be nearly at those sandhills by now,' his heart leaped into his mouth because an appalling noise had suddenly risen up out of the darkness ahead; a long snarling roar, melancholy and utterly savage.

Instantly Bree swerved round and began galloping inland again as fast as he could gallop.

'What is it?' gasped Shasta.

'Lions!' said Bree, without checking his pace or turning his head.

After that there was nothing but sheer galloping for some time. At last they splashed across a wide, shallow stream and Bree came to a stop on the far side. Shasta noticed that he was trembling and sweating all over.

'That water may have thrown the brute off our scent,' panted Bree when he had partly got his breath again. 'We can walk for a bit now.'

As they walked Bree said, 'Shasta, I'm ashamed of myself. I'm just as frightened as a common, dumb Calormene horse. I am really. I don't feel like a Talking Horse at all. I don't mind swords and lances and arrows but I can't bear – those creatures. I think I'll trot for a bit.'

About a minute later, however, he broke into a gallop again, and no wonder. For the roar broke out again, this time on their left from the direction of the forest.

'Two of them,' moaned Bree.

When they had galloped for several minutes without any further noise from the lions Shasta said, 'I say! That other horse is galloping beside us now. Only a stone's throw away.'

'All the b-better,' panted Bree. 'Tarkaan on it – will have a sword – protect us all.'

'But, Bree!' said Shasta. 'We might just as well be killed by lions as caught. Or I might. They'll hang me for horse-stealing.' He was feeling less frightened of lions than Bree because he had never met a lion; Bree had.

Bree only snorted in answer but he did sheer away to

his right. Oddly enough the other horse seemed also to be sheering away to the left, so that in a few seconds the space between them had widened a good deal. But as soon as it did so there came two more lions' roars, immediately after one another, one on the right and the other on the left, and the horses began drawing nearer together. So, apparently, did the lions. The roaring of the brutes on each side was horribly close and they seemed to be keeping

up with the galloping horses quite easily. Then the cloud rolled away. The moonlight, astonishingly bright, showed up everything almost as if it were broad day. The two horses and the two riders were galloping neck to neck and knee to knee just as if they were in a race. Indeed Bree said (afterwards) that a finer race had never been seen in Calormen.

Shasta now gave himself up for lost and began to wonder whether lions killed you quickly or played with you as a cat plays with a mouse and how much it would hurt. At

the same time (one sometimes does this at the most frightful moments) he noticed everything. He saw that the
other rider was a very small, slender person, mail-clad (the
moon shone on the mail) and riding magnificently. He had
no beard.

Something flat and shining was spread out before them.
Before Shasta had time even to guess what it was there was
a great splash and he found his mouth half full of salt water.
The shining thing had been a long inlet of the sea. Both
horses were swimming and the water was up to Shasta's
knees. There was an angry roaring behind them and looking back Shasta saw a great, shaggy, and terrible shape
crouched on the water's edge; but only one. 'We must
have shaken off the other lion,' he thought.

The lion apparently did not think its prey worth a wet-
ting; at any rate it made no attempt to take the water in
pursuit. The two horses, side by side, were now well out
into the middle of the creek and the opposite shore could
be clearly seen. The Tarkaan had not yet spoken a word.
'But he will,' thought Shasta. 'As soon as we have landed.
What am I to say? I must begin thinking out a story.'

Then, suddenly, two voices spoke at his side.

'Oh, I *am* so tired,' said the one.

'Hold your tongue, Hwin, and don't be a fool,' said
the other.

'I'm dreaming,' thought Shasta. 'I could have sworn
that other horse spoke.'

Soon the horses were no longer swimming but walking
and soon with a great sound of water running off their sides
and tails and with a great crunching of pebbles under eight
hoofs, they came out on the farther beach of the inlet. The
Tarkaan, to Shasta's surprise, showed no wish to ask

questions. He did not even look at Shasta but seemed anxious to urge his horse straight on. Bree, however, at once shouldered himself in the other horse's way.

'Broo-hoo-hah!' he snorted. 'Steady there! I *heard* you, I did. There's no good pretending, Ma'am. *I* heard you. You're a Talking Horse, a Narnian horse just like me.'

'What's it got to do with you if she is?' said the strange rider fiercely, laying hand on sword-hilt. But the voice in which the words were spoken had already told Shasta something.

'Why, it's only a girl!' he exclaimed.

'And what business is it of yours if I am *only* a girl?' snapped the stranger. 'You're only a boy: a rude, common little boy – a slave probably, who's stolen his master's horse.'

'That's all *you* know,' said Shasta.

'He's not a thief, little Tarkheena,' said Bree. 'At least, if there's been any stealing, you might just as well say I stole *him*. And as for its not being my business, you wouldn't expect me to pass a lady of my own race in this strange country without speaking to her? It's only natural I should.'

'I think it's very natural too,' said the mare.

'I wish you'd held your tongue, Hwin,' said the girl. 'Look at the trouble you've got us into.'

'I don't know about trouble,' said Shasta. 'You can clear off as soon as you like. We shan't keep you.'

'No, you shan't,' said the girl.

'What quarrelsome creatures these humans are,' said Bree to the mare. 'They're as bad as mules. Let's try to talk a little sense. I take it, Ma'am, your story is the same as mine? Captured in early youth – years of slavery among the Calormenes?'

'Too true, sir,' said the mare with a melancholy whinny.

'And now, perhaps – escape?'

'Tell him to mind his own business, Hwin,' said the girl.

'No, I won't, Aravis,' said the mare, putting her ears back. 'This is my escape just as much as yours. And I'm sure a noble war-horse like this is not going to betray us. We are trying to escape, to get to Narnia.'

'And so, of course, are we,' said Bree. 'Of course you guessed that at once. A little boy in rags riding (or trying to ride) a war-horse at dead of night couldn't mean anything but an escape of some sort. And, if I may say so, a high-born Tarkheena riding alone at night – dressed up in her brother's armour – and very anxious for everyone to mind their own business and ask her no questions – well, if that's not fishy, call me a cob!'

'All right then,' said Aravis. 'You've guessed it. Hwin and I are running away. We are trying to get to Narnia. And now, what about it?'

'Why, in that case, what is to prevent us all going together?' said Bree. 'I trust, Madam Hwin, you will accept such assistance and protection as I may be able to give you on the journey?'

'Why do you keep on talking to my horse instead of to me?' asked the girl.

'Excuse me, Tarkheena,' said Bree (with just the slightest backward tilt of his ears), 'but that's Calormene talk. We're free Narnians, Hwin and I, and I suppose, if you're running away to Narnia, you want to be one too. In that case Hwin isn't *your* horse any longer. One might just as well say you're *her* human.'

The girl opened her mouth to speak and then stopped. Obviously she had not quite seen it in that light before.

'Still,' she said after a moment's pause, 'I don't know that there's so much point in all going together. Aren't we more likely to be noticed?'

'Less,' said Bree; and the mare said, 'Oh do let's. I should feel much more comfortable. We're not even certain of the way. I'm sure a great charger like this knows far more than we do.'

'Oh come on, Bree,' said Shasta, 'and let them go their own way. Can't you see they don't want us?'

'We do,' said Hwin.

'Look here,' said the girl. 'I don't mind going with *you*, Mr War-Horse, but what about this boy? How do I know he's not a spy?'

'Why don't you say at once that you think I'm not good enough for you?' said Shasta.

'Be quiet, Shasta,' said Bree. 'The Tarkheena's question is quite reasonable. I'll vouch for the boy, Tarkheena. He's been true to me and a good friend. And he's certainly either a Narnian or an Archenlander.'

'All right, then. Let's go together.' But she didn't say anything to Shasta and it was obvious that she wanted Bree, not him.

'Splendid!' said Bree. 'And now that we've got the water between us and those dreadful animals, what about you two humans taking off our saddles and our all having a rest and hearing one another's stories.'

Both the children unsaddled their horses and the horses had a little grass and Aravis produced rather nice things to eat from her saddle-bag. But Shasta sulked and said No thanks, and that he wasn't hungry. And he tried to put on what he thought very grand and stiff manners, but as a fisherman's hut is not usually a good place for learning grand manners, the result was dreadful. And he half knew that it wasn't a success and then became sulkier and more awkward than ever. Meanwhile the two horses were getting on splendidly. They remembered the very same places in Narnia – 'the grasslands up above Beaversdam' and found that they were some sort of second cousins once removed. This made things more and more uncomfortable for the humans until at last Bree said, 'And now, Tarkheena, tell us your story. And don't hurry it – I'm feeling comfortable now.'

Aravis immediately began, sitting quite still and using a rather different tone and style from her usual one. For in Calormen, story-telling (whether the stories are true or made up) is a thing you're taught, just as English boys and girls are taught essay-writing. The difference is that people want to hear the stories, whereas I never heard of anyone who wanted to read the essays.

CHAPTER 3

AT THE GATES OF TASHBAAN

'My name,' said the girl at once, 'is Aravis Tarkheena and I am the only daughter of Kidrash Tarkaan, the son of Rishti Tarkaan, the son of Kidrash Tarkaan, the son of Ilsombreh Tisroc, the son of Ardeeb Tisroc who was descended in a right line from the god Tash. My father is lord of the province of Calavar and is one who has the right of standing on his feet in his shoes before the face of the Tisroc himself (may he live for ever). My mother (on whom be the peace of the gods) is dead and my father has married another wife. One of my brothers has fallen in battle against the rebels in the far west and the other is a child. Now it came to pass that my father's wife, my step-mother, hated me, and the sun appeared dark in her eyes as long as I lived in my father's house. And so she persuaded my father to promise me in marriage to Ahoshta Tarkaan. Now this Ahoshta is of base birth, though in these latter years he has won the favour of the Tisroc (may he live for ever) by flattery and evil counsels, and is now made a Tarkaan and lord of many cities and is likely to be chosen as the Grand Vizier when the present Grand Vizier dies. Moreover he is at least sixty years old and has a hump on his back and his face resembles that of an ape. Nevertheless my father, because of the wealth and power of this Ahoshta, and being persuaded by his wife, sent messengers offering me in marriage, and the offer was favourably accepted and Ahoshta sent word that he would marry me this very year at the time of high summer.

'When this news was brought to me the sun appeared dark in my eyes and I laid myself on my bed and wept for a day. But on the second day I rose up and washed my face and caused my mare Hwin to be saddled and took with me a sharp dagger which my brother had carried in the western wars and rode out alone. And when my father's house was out of sight and I was come to a green open place in a certain wood where there were no dwellings of men, I dismounted from Hwin my mare and took out the dagger. Then I parted my clothes where I thought the readiest way lay to my heart and I prayed to all the gods that as soon as I was dead I might find myself with my brother. After that I shut my eyes and my teeth and prepared to drive the dagger into my heart. But before I had done so, this mare spoke with the voice of one of the daughters of men and said, "O my mistress, do not by any means destroy yourself, for if you live you may yet have good fortune but all the dead are dead alike."'

'I didn't say it half so well as that,' muttered the mare.

'Hush, Ma'am, hush,' said Bree, who was thoroughly enjoying the story. 'She's telling it in the grand Calormene manner and no story-teller in a Tisroc's court could do it better. Pray go on, Tarkheena.'

'When I heard the language of men uttered by my mare,' continued Aravis, 'I said to myself, the fear of death has disordered my reason and subjected me to delusions. And I became full of shame for none of my lineage ought to fear death more than the biting of a gnat. Therefore I addressed myself a second time to the stabbing, but Hwin came near to me and put her head in between me and the dagger and discoursed to me most excellent reasons and rebuked me as a mother rebukes her daughter. And now my wonder was so great that I forgot about killing myself and about Ahoshta and said, "O my mare, how have you learned to speak like one of the daughters of men?" And Hwin told me what is known to all this company, that in Narnia there are beasts that talk, and how she herself was stolen from thence when she was a little foal. She told me also of the woods and waters of Narnia and the castles and the great ships, till I said, "In the name of Tash and Azaroth and Zardeenah Lady of the Night, I have a great wish to be in that country of Narnia." "O my mistress," answered the mare, "if you were in Narnia you would be happy, for in that land no maiden is forced to marry against her will."

'And when we had talked together for a great time hope returned to me and I rejoiced that I had not killed myself. Moreover it was agreed between Hwin and me that we should steal ourselves away together and we planned it in this fashion. We returned to my father's house and I put on my gayest clothes and sang and danced before my father and pretended to be delighted with the marriage which he had prepared for me. Also I said to him, "O my father and O the delight of my eyes, give me your licence and permission to go with one of my maidens alone for three days into the woods to do secret sacrifices to Zardeenah, Lady of the Night and of Maidens, as is proper and customary for damsels when they must bid farewell to the service of Zardeenah and prepare themselves for marriage." And he answered, "O my daughter and O the delight of my eyes, so shall it be."

'But when I came out from the presence of my father I went immediately to the oldest of his slaves, his secretary, who had dandled me on his knees when I was a baby and loved me more than the air and the light. And I swore him to be secret and begged him to write a certain letter for me. And he wept and implored me to change my resolution but in the end he said, "To hear is to obey," and did all my will. And I sealed the letter and hid it in my bosom.'

'But what was in the letter?' asked Shasta.

'Be quiet, youngster,' said Bree. 'You're spoiling the story. She'll tell us all about the letter in the right place. Go on, Tarkheena.'

'Then I called the maid who was to go with me to the woods and perform the rites of Zardeenah and told her to wake me very early in the morning. And I became merry with her and gave her wine to drink; but I had mixed such things in her cup that I knew she must sleep for a night and a day. As soon as the household of my father had committed themselves to sleep I arose and put on an armour of my brother's which I always kept in my chamber in his memory. I put into my girdle all the money I had and certain choice jewels and provided myself also with food, and saddled the mare with my own hands and rode away in the second watch of the night. I directed my course not to the woods where my father supposed that I would go but north and east to Tashbaan.

'Now for three days and more I knew that my father would not seek me, being deceived by the words I had said to him. And on the fourth day we arrived at the city of Azim Balda. Now Azim Balda stands at the meeting of many roads and from it the posts of the Tisroc (may he live for ever) ride on swift horses to every part of the empire: and it is one of the rights and privileges of the greater Tarkaans to send messages by them. I therefore went to the Chief of the Messengers in the House of Imperial Posts in Azim Balda and said, "O dispatcher of messages,

here is a letter from my uncle Ahoshta Tarkaan to Kidrash Tarkaan lord of Calavar. Take now these five crescents and cause it to be sent to him." And the Chief of the Messengers said, "To hear is to obey."

'This letter was feigned to be written by Ahoshta and this was the signification of the writing: "Ahoshta Tarkaan to Kidrash Tarkaan, salutation and peace. In the name of Tash the irresistible, the inexorable. Be it known to you that as I made my journey towards your house to perform the contract of marriage between me and your daughter Aravis Tarkheena, it pleased fortune and the gods that I fell in with her in the forest when she had ended the rites and sacrifices of Zardeenah according to the custom of maidens. And when I learned who she was, being delighted with her beauty and discretion, I became inflamed with love and it appeared to me that the sun would be dark to me if I did not marry her at once. Accordingly I prepared the necessary sacrifices and married your daughter the same hour that I met her and have returned

with her to my own house. And we both pray and charge
you to come hither as speedily as you may that we may be
delighted with your face and speech; and also that you may
bring with you the dowry of my wife, which, by reason of
my great charges and expenses, I require without delay.
And because thou and I are as brothers I assure myself
that you will not be angered by the haste of my marriage
which is wholly occasioned by the great love I bear your
daughter. And I commit you to the care of all the gods.'

'As soon as I had done this I rode on in all haste from
Azim Balda, fearing no pursuit and expecting that my
father, having received such a letter, would send messages
to Ahoshta or go to him himself, and that before the
matter was discovered I should be beyond Tashbaan. And
that is the pith of my story until this very night when I was
chased by lions and met you at the swimming of the salt
water.'

'And what happened to the girl – the one you drugged?'
asked Shasta.

'Doubtless she was beaten for sleeping late,' said Aravis
coolly. 'But she was a tool and spy of my stepmother's. I
am very glad they should beat her.'

'I say, that was hardly fair,' said Shasta.

'I did not do any of these things for the sake of pleasing
you,' said Aravis.

'And there's another thing I don't understand about that
story,' said Shasta. 'You're not grown up, I don't believe
you're any older than I am. I don't believe you're as old.
How could you be getting married at your age?'

Aravis said nothing, but Bree at once said, 'Shasta, don't
display your ignorance. They're always married at that age
in the great Tarkaan families.'

Shasta turned very red (though it was hardly light enough for the others to see this) and felt snubbed. Aravis asked Bree for his story. Bree told it, and Shasta thought that he put in a great deal more than he needed about the falls and the bad riding. Bree obviously thought it very funny, but Aravis did not laugh. When Bree had finished they all went to sleep.

Next day all four of them, two horses and two humans, continued their journey together. Shasta thought it had been much pleasanter when he and Bree were on their own. For now it was Bree and Aravis who did nearly all the talking. Bree had lived a long time in Calormen and had always been among Tarkaans and Tarkaans' horses, and so of course he knew a great many of the same people and places that Aravis knew. She would always be saying things like, 'But if you were at the fight of Zulindreh you would have seen my cousin Alimash,' and Bree would answer, 'Oh, yes, Alimash, he was only captain of the chariots, you know. I don't quite hold with chariots or the kind of horses who draw chariots. That's not real cavalry. But he is a worthy nobleman. He filled my nosebag with sugar after the taking of Teebeth.' Or else Bree would say, 'I was down at the lake of Mezreel that summer,' and Aravis would say, 'Oh, Mezreel! I had a friend there, Lasaraleen Tarkheena. What a delightful place it is. Those gardens, and the Valley of the Thousand Perfumes!' Bree was not in the least trying to leave Shasta out of things, though Shasta sometimes nearly thought he was. People who know a lot of the same things can hardly help talking about them, and if you're there you can hardly help feeling that you're out of it.

Hwin the mare was rather shy before a great war-horse

like Bree and said very little. And Aravis never spoke to Shasta at all if she could help it.

Soon, however, they had more important things to think of. They were getting near Tashbaan. There were more, and larger, villages, and more people on the roads. They now did nearly all their travelling by night and hid as best they could during the day. And at every halt they argued and argued about what they were to do when they reached Tashbaan. Everyone had been putting off this difficulty, but now it could be put off no longer. During these discussions Aravis became a little, a very little, less unfriendly to Shasta; one usually gets on better with people when one is making plans than when one is talking about nothing in particular.

Bree said the first thing now to do was to fix a place where they would all promise to meet on the far side of Tashbaan even if, by any ill luck, they got separated in passing the city. He said the best place would be the Tombs of the Ancient Kings on the very edge of the desert. 'Things like great stone bee-hives,' he said, 'you can't possibly miss them. And the best of it is that none of the Calormenes will go near them because they think the place is haunted by ghouls and are afraid of it.' Aravis asked if it wasn't really haunted by ghouls. But Bree said he was a free Narnian horse and didn't believe in these Calormene tales. And then Shasta said he wasn't a Calormene either and didn't care a straw about these old stories of ghouls. This wasn't quite true. But it rather impressed Aravis (though at the moment it annoyed her too) and of course she said she didn't mind any number of ghouls either. So it was settled that the Tombs should be their assembly place on the other side of Tashbaan, and everyone felt they

were getting on very well till Hwin humbly pointed out
that the real problem was not where they should go when
they had got through Tashbaan but how they were to get
through it.

'We'll settle that tomorrow, Ma'am,' said Bree. 'Time
for a little sleep now.'

But it wasn't easy to settle. Aravis's first suggestion was
that they should swim across the river below the city
during the night and not go into Tashbaan at all. But Bree
had two reasons against this. One was that the river-mouth
was very wide and it would be far too long a swim for
Hwin to do, especially with a rider on her back. (He
thought it would be too long for himself too, but he said
much less about that.) The other was that it would be full
of shipping and of course anyone on the deck of a ship
who saw two horses swimming past would be almost
certain to be inquisitive.

Shasta thought they should go up the river above
Tashbaan and cross it where it was narrower. But Bree
explained that there were gardens and pleasure houses on
both banks of the river for miles and that there would be
Tarkaans and Tarkheenas living in them and riding about
the roads and having water parties on the river. In fact it
would be the most likely place in the world for meeting
someone who would recognize Aravis or even himself.

'We'll have to have a disguise,' said Shasta.

Hwin said it looked to her as if the safest thing was to
go right through the city itself from gate to gate because
one was less likely to be noticed in the crowd. But she
approved of the idea of disguise as well. She said, 'Both
the humans will have to dress in rags and look like peasants or slaves. And all Aravis's armour and our saddles and

things must be made into bundles and put on our backs, and the children must pretend to drive us and people will think we're only pack-horses.'

'My dear Hwin!' said Aravis rather scornfully. 'As if anyone could mistake Bree for anything but a war-horse however you disguised him!'

'I should think not, indeed,' said Bree, snorting and letting his ears go ever so little back.

'I know it's not a *very* good plan,' said Hwin. 'But I think it's our only chance. And we haven't been groomed for ages and we're not looking quite ourselves (at least, I'm sure I'm not). I do think if we get well plastered with mud and go along with our heads down as if we're tired and lazy – and don't lift our hooves hardly at all – we might not be noticed. And our tails ought to be cut shorter: not neatly, you know, but all ragged.'

'My dear Madam,' said Bree. 'Have you pictured to yourself how very disagreeable it would be to arrive in Narnia in *that* condition?'

'Well,' said Hwin humbly (she was a very sensible mare), 'the main thing is to get there.'

Though nobody much liked it, it was Hwin's plan which had to be adopted in the end. It was a troublesome one and involved a certain amount of what Shasta called stealing, and Bree called 'raiding'. One farm lost a few sacks that evening and another lost a coil of rope the next: but some tattered old boy's clothes for Aravis to wear had to be fairly bought and paid for in a village. Shasta returned with them in triumph just as evening was closing in. The others were waiting for him among the trees at the foot of a low range of wooded hills which lay right across their path. Everyone was feeling excited because this was the last hill; when they reached the ridge at the top they would be looking down on Tashbaan. 'I do wish we were safely past it,' muttered Shasta to Hwin. 'Oh I do, I do,' said Hwin fervently.

That night they wound their way through the woods up to the ridge by a wood-cutter's track. And when they came out of the woods at the top they could see thousands of lights in the valley down below them. Shasta had had no notion of what a great city would be like and it frightened him. They had their supper and the children got some sleep. But the horses woke them very early in the morning.

The stars were still out and the grass was terribly cold and wet, but daybreak was just beginning, far to their right across the sea. Aravis went a few steps away into the wood and came back looking odd in her new, ragged clothes and carrying her real ones in a bundle. These, and her armour and shield and scimitar and the two saddles and the rest of the horses' fine furnishings were put into the sacks. Bree and Hwin had already got themselves as dirty and bedraggled as they could and it only remained to shorten their tails. As the only tool for doing this was Aravis's scimitar, one of the packs had to be undone again in order to get it out. It was a longish job and rather hurt the horses.

'My word!' said Bree, 'if I wasn't a Talking Horse what a lovely kick in the face I could give you! I thought you were going to cut it, not pull it out. That's what it feels like.'

But in spite of semi-darkness and cold fingers all was done in the end, the big packs bound on the horses, the rope halters (which they were now wearing instead of bridles and reins) in the children's hands, and the journey began.

'Remember,' said Bree. 'Keep together if we possibly can. If not, meet at the Tombs of the Ancient Kings, and whoever gets there first must wait for the others.'

'And remember,' said Shasta. 'Don't you two horses forget yourselves and start *talking*, whatever happens.'

CHAPTER 4

SHASTA FALLS IN WITH THE NARNIANS

AT first Shasta could see nothing in the valley below him but a sea of mist with a few domes and pinnacles rising from it; but as the light increased and the mist cleared away he saw more and more. A broad river divided itself into two streams and on the island between them stood the city of Tashbaan, one of the wonders of the world. Round the very edge of the island, so that the water lapped against the stone, ran high walls strengthened with so many towers that he soon gave up trying to count them. Inside the walls the island rose in a hill and every bit of that hill, up to the Tisroc's palace and the great temple of Tash at the top, was completely covered with buildings – terrace above terrace, street above street, zigzag roads or huge flights of steps bordered with orange trees and lemon trees, roof-gardens, balconies, deep archways, pillared colonnades, spires, battlements, minarets, pinnacles. And when at last the sun rose out of the sea and the great silver-plated dome of the temple flashed back its light, he was almost dazzled.

'Get on, Shasta,' Bree kept saying.

The river banks on each side of the valley were such a mass of gardens that they looked at first like forest, until you got closer and saw the white walls of innumerable houses peeping out from beneath the trees. Soon after that, Shasta noticed a delicious smell of flowers and fruit. About fifteen minutes later they were down among them,

plodding on a level road with white walls on each side and
trees bending over the walls.

'I say,' said Shasta in an awed voice. 'This is a wonderful
place!'

'I daresay,' said Bree. 'But I wish we were safely through
it and out at the other side. Narnia and the North!'

At that moment a low, throbbing noise began which
gradually swelled louder and louder till the whole valley
seemed to be swaying with it. It was a musical noise, but so
strong and solemn as to be a little frightening.

'That's the horns blowing for the city gates to be open,'
said Bree. 'We shall be there in a minute. Now, Aravis, do
droop your shoulders a bit and step heavier and try to look
less like a princess. Try to imagine you've been kicked and
cuffed and called names all your life.'

'If it comes to that,' said Aravis, 'what about you droop-
ing your head a bit more and arching your neck a bit less
and trying to look less like a war-horse?'

'Hush,' said Bree. 'Here we are.'

And they were. They had come to the river's edge and
the road ahead of them ran along a many-arched bridge.

The water danced brightly in the early sunlight; away to their right nearer the river's mouth, they caught a glimpse of ships' masts. Several other travellers were before them on the bridge, mostly peasants driving laden donkeys and mules or carrying baskets on their heads. The children and the horses joined the crowd.

'Is anything wrong?' whispered Shasta to Aravis, who had an odd look on her face.

'Oh it's all very well for *you*,' whispered Aravis rather savagely. 'What do *you* care about Tashbaan? But I ought to be riding in on a litter with soldiers before me and slaves behind, and perhaps going to a great feast in the Tisroc's palace (may he live for ever) – not sneaking in like this. It's different for you.'

Shasta thought all this very silly.

At the far end of the bridge the walls of the city towered high above them and the brazen gates stood open in the gateway which was really wide but looked narrow because it was so very high. Half a dozen soldiers, leaning on their spears, stood on each side. Aravis couldn't help thinking, 'They'd all jump to attention and salute me if they knew whose daughter I am.' But the others were only thinking of how they'd get through and hoping the soldiers would not ask any questions. Fortunately they did not. But one of them picked a carrot out of a peasant's basket and threw it at Shasta with a rough laugh, saying:

'Hey! Horse-boy! You'll catch it if your master finds you've been using his saddle-horse for pack work.'

This frightened him badly for of course it showed that no one who knew anything about horses would mistake Bree for anything but a charger.

'It's my master's orders, so there!' said Shasta. But it

would have been better if he had held his tongue for the soldier gave him a box on the side of his face that nearly knocked him down and said, 'Take that, you young filth, to teach you how to talk to freemen.' But they all slunk into the city without being stopped. Shasta cried only a very little; he was used to hard knocks.

Inside the gates Tashbaan did not at first seem so splendid as it had looked from a distance. The first street was narrow and there were hardly any windows in the walls on each side. It was much more crowded than Shasta had expected: crowded partly by the peasants (on their way to market) who had come in with them, but also with water-sellers, sweetmeat sellers, porters, soldiers, beggars, ragged children, hens, stray dogs, and bare-footed slaves. What you would chiefly have noticed if you had been there was the smells, which came from unwashed people, unwashed dogs, scent, garlic, onions, and the piles of refuse which lay everywhere.

Shasta was pretending to lead but it was really Bree, who knew the way and kept guiding him by little nudges with his nose. They soon turned to the left and began going up a steep hill. It was much fresher and pleasanter, for the road was bordered by trees and there were houses only on the right side; on the other they looked out over the roofs of houses in the lower town and could see some way up the river. Then they went round a hairpin bend to their right and continued rising. They were zigzagging up to the centre of Tashbaan. Soon they came to finer streets. Great statues of the gods and heroes of Calormen – who are mostly impressive rather than agreeable to look at – rose on shining pedestals. Palm trees and pillared arcades cast shadows over the burning pavements. And through the arched gateways of many a palace Shasta caught sight of green branches, cool fountains, and smooth lawns. It must be nice inside, he thought.

At every turn Shasta hoped they were getting out of the crowd, but they never did. This made their progress very slow, and every now and then they had to stop altogether. This usually happened because a loud voice shouted out 'Way, way way, for the Tarkaan', or 'for the Tarkheena', or 'for the fifteenth Vizier', or 'for the Ambassador', and everyone in the crowd would crush back against the walls; and above their heads Shasta would sometimes see the great lord or lady for whom all the fuss was being made, lolling upon a litter which four or even six gigantic slaves carried on their bare shoulders. For in Tashbaan there is only one traffic regulation, which is that everyone who is less important has to get out of the way for everyone who is more important; unless you want a cut from a whip or a punch from the butt end of a spear.

It was in a splendid street very near the top of the city (the Tisroc's palace was the only thing above it) that the most disastrous of these stoppages occurred.

'Way! Way! Way!' came the voice. 'Way for the White Barbarian King, the guest of the Tisroc (may he live for ever)! Way for the Narnian lords.'

Shasta tried to get out of the way and to make Bree go back. But no horse, not even a talking Horse from Narnia, backs easily. And a woman with a very edgy basket in her hands, who was just behind Shasta, pushed the basket hard against his shoulders, and said, 'Now then! Who are you shoving!' And then someone else jostled him from the side and in the confusion of the moment he lost hold of Bree. And then the whole crowd behind him became so stiffened and packed tight that he couldn't move at all. So he found himself, unintentionally, in the first row and had a fine sight of the party that was coming down the street.

It was quite unlike any other party they had seen that day. The crier who went before it shouting 'Way, way!' was the only Calormene in it. And there was no litter; everyone was on foot. There were about half a dozen men and Shasta had never seen anyone like them before. For one thing, they were all as fair-skinned as himself, and most of them had fair hair. And they were not dressed like men of Calormen. Most of them had legs bare to the knee. Their tunics were of fine, bright, hardy colours – woodland green, or gay yellow, or fresh blue. Instead of turbans they wore steel or silver caps, some of them set with jewels, and one with little wings on each side of it. A few were bare-headed. The swords at their sides were long and straight, not curved like Calormene scimitars. And instead of being grave and mysterious like most Calormenes, they walked with a swing and let their arms and shoulders go free, and chatted and laughed. One was whistling. You could see that they were ready to be friends with anyone who was friendly and didn't give a fig for anyone who wasn't. Shasta thought he had never seen anything so lovely in his life.

But there was no time to enjoy it for at once a really dreadful thing happened. The leader of the fair-headed men suddenly pointed at Shasta, cried out, 'There he is! There's our runaway!' and seized him by the shoulder. Next moment he gave Shasta a smack – not a cruel one to make you cry but a sharp one to let you know you are in disgrace – and added, shaking him:

'Shame on you, my lord! Fie for shame! Queen Susan's

eyes are red with weeping because of you. What! Truant
for a whole night! Where have you been?'

Shasta would have darted under Bree's body and tried
to make himself scarce in the crowd if he had had the least
chance; but the fair-haired men were all round him by
now and he was held firm.

Of course his first impulse was to say that he was only
poor Arsheesh the fisherman's son and that the foreign
lord must have mistaken him for someone else. But then,
the very last thing he wanted to do in that crowded place
was to start explaining who he was and what he was doing.
If he started on that, he would soon be asked where he had
got his horse from, and who Aravis was – and then, good-
bye to any chance of getting through Tashbaan. His next
impulse was to look at Bree for help. But Bree had no
intention of letting all that crowd know that he could talk,
and stood looking just as stupid as a horse can. As for
Aravis, Shasta did not even dare to look at her for fear of
drawing attention. And there was no time to think, for
the leader of the Narnians said at once:

'Take one of his little lordship's hands, Peridan, of
your courtesy and I'll take the other. And now, on. Our
royal sister's mind will be greatly eased when she sees our
young scapegrace safe in our lodging.'

And so, before they were half-way through Tashbaan,
all their plans were ruined, and without even a chance to
say good-bye to the others Shasta found himself being
marched off among strangers and quite unable to guess
what might be going to happen next. The Narnian King
– for Shasta began to see by the way the rest spoke to him
that he must be a king – kept on asking him questions;
where he had been, how he had got out, what he had done

with his clothes, and didn't he know that he had been very naughty. Only the king called it 'naught' instead of naughty.

And Shasta said nothing in answer, because he couldn't think of anything to say that would not be dangerous.

'What! All mum?' asked the king. 'I must plainly tell you, prince, that this hangdog silence becomes one of your blood even less than the scape itself. To run away might pass for a boy's frolic with some spirit in it. But the king's son of Archenland should avouch his deed: not hang his head like a Calormene slave.'

This was very unpleasant, for Shasta felt all the time that this young king was the very nicest kind of grown-up and would have liked to make a good impression on him.

The strangers led him – held tightly by both hands – along a narrow street and down a flight of shallow stairs and then up another to a wide doorway in a white wall with two tall, dark cypress trees, one on each side of it. Once through the arch, Shasta found himself in a courtyard which was also a garden. A marble basin of clear water in the centre was kept continually rippling by the fountain that fell into it. Orange trees grew round it out of smooth grass, and the four white walls which surrounded the lawn were covered with climbing roses. The noise and dust and crowding of the streets seemed suddenly far away. He was led rapidly across the garden and then into a dark doorway. The crier remained outside. After that they took him along a corridor, where the stone floor felt beautifully cool to his hot feet, and up some stairs. A moment later he found himself blinking in the light of a big, airy room with wide open windows, all looking North so that no sun came in. There was a carpet on the floor more wonderfully coloured than anything he had ever seen and his feet sank down into it as if he were treading in thick moss. All round the walls there were low sofas with rich cushions on them, and the room seemed to be full of people; very queer people some of them, thought Shasta. But he had no time to think of that before the most beautiful lady he had ever seen rose from her place and threw her arms round him and kissed him, saying:

'Oh Corin, Corin, how could you? And thou and I such close friends ever since thy mother died. And what should I have said to thy royal father if I came home without thee? Would have been a cause almost of war between Archenland and Narnia which are friends time out of mind. It was naught, playmate, very naught of thee to use us so.'

'Apparently,' thought Shasta to himself, 'I'm being mistaken for a prince of Archenland, wherever that is. And these must be the Narnians. I wonder where the real Corin is?' But these thoughts did not help him to say anything out loud.

'Where hast been, Corin?' said the lady, her hands still on Shasta's shoulders.

'I – I don't know,' stammered Shasta.

'There it is, Susan,' said the King. 'I could get no tale out of him, true or false.'

'Your Majesties! Queen Susan! King Edmund!' said a voice: and when Shasta turned to look at the speaker he nearly jumped out of his skin with surprise. For this was one of those queer people whom he had noticed out of the corner of his eye when he first came into the room. He was about the same height as Shasta himself. From the waist upwards he was like a man, but his legs were hairy

like a goat's, and shaped like a goat's and he had goat's
hooves and a tail. His skin was rather red and he had curly
hair and a short pointed beard and two little horns. He
was in fact a Faun, which is a creature Shasta had never
seen a picture of or even heard of. And if you've read a
book called *The Lion, the Witch, and the Wardrobe* you may
like to know that this was the very same Faun, Tumnus by
name, whom Queen Susan's sister Lucy had met on the
very first day when she found her way into Narnia. But he
was a good deal older now for by this time Peter and Susan
and Edmund and Lucy had been Kings and Queens of
Narnia for several years.

'Your Majesties,' he was saying, 'His little Highness has
had a touch of the sun. Look at him! He is dazed. He does
not know where he is.'

Then of course everyone stopped scolding Shasta and
asking him questions and he was made much of and laid on
a sofa and cushions were put under his head and he was
given iced sherbet in a golden cup to drink and told to keep
very quiet.

Nothing like this had ever happened to Shasta in his life
before. He had never even imagined lying on anything so
comfortable as that sofa or drinking anything so delicious
as that sherbet. He was still wondering what had happened
to the others and how on earth he was going to escape and
meet them at the Tombs, and what would happen when the
real Corin turned up again. But none of these worries
seemed so pressing now that he was comfortable. And
perhaps, later on, there would be nice things to eat!

Meanwhile the people in that cool, airy room were very
interesting. Besides the Faun there were two Dwarfs (a
kind of creature he had never seen before) and a very large

Raven. The rest were all humans; grown-ups, but young, and all of them, both men and women, had nicer faces and voices than most Calormenes. And soon Shasta found himself taking an interest in the conversation.

'Now, Madam,' the King was saying to Queen Susan (the lady who had kissed Shasta). 'What think you? We have been in this city fully three weeks. Have you yet

settled in your mind whether you will marry this dark-faced lover of yours, this Prince Rabadash, or no?'

The lady shook her head. 'No, brother,' she said, 'not for all the jewels in Tashbaan.' ('Hullo!' thought Shasta. 'Although they're king and queen, they're brother and sister, not married to one another.')

'Truly, sister,' said the King, 'I should have loved you the less if you had taken him. And I tell you that at the first coming of the Tisroc's ambassadors into Narnia to treat of this marriage, and later when the Prince was our guest at Cair Paravel, it was a wonder to me that ever you could find it in your heart to show him so much favour.'

'That was my folly, Edmund,' said Queen Susan, 'of which I cry you mercy. Yet when he was with us in Narnia, truly this Prince bore himself in another fashion than he does now in Tashbaan. For I take you all to witness what marvellous feats he did in that great tournament and hasti-lude which our brother the High King made for him, and how meekly and courteously he consorted with us the space of seven days. But here, in his own city, he has shown another face.'

'Ah!' croaked the Raven. 'It is an old saying: see the bear in his own den before you judge of his conditions.'

'That's very true, Sallowpad,' said one of the Dwarfs. 'And another is, Come, live with me and you'll know me.'

'Yes,' said the King. 'We have now seen him for what he is: that is, a most proud, bloody, luxurious, cruel, and self-pleasing tyrant.'

'Then in the name of Aslan,' said Susan, 'let us leave Tashbaan this very day.'

'There's the rub, sister,' said Edmund. 'For now I must open to you all that has been growing in my mind these last two days and more. Peridan, of your courtesy look to the door and see that there is no spy upon us. All well? So. For now we must be secret.'

Everyone had begun to look very serious. Queen Susan jumped up and ran to her brother. 'Oh, Edmund,' she cried. 'What is it? There is something dreadful in your face.'

CHAPTER 5

PRINCE CORIN

'My dear sister and very good Lady,' said King Edmund, 'you must now show your courage. For I tell you plainly we are in no small danger.'

'What is it, Edmund?' asked the Queen.

'It is this,' said Edmund. 'I do not think we shall find it easy to leave Tashbaan. While the Prince had hope that you would take him, we were honoured guests. But by the Lion's Mane, I think that as soon as he has your flat denial we shall be no better than prisoners.'

One of the Dwarfs gave a low whistle.

'I warned your Majesties, I warned you,' said Sallow-pad the Raven. 'Easily in but not easily out, as the lobster said in the lobster pot!'

'I have been with the Prince this morning,' continued Edmund. 'He is little used (more's the pity) to having his will crossed. And he is very chafed at your long delays and doubtful answers. This morning he pressed very hard to know your mind. I put it aside – meaning at the same time to diminish his hopes – with some light common jests about women's fancies, and hinted that his suit was likely to be cold. He grew angry and dangerous. There was a sort of threatening, though still veiled under a show of courtesy, in every word he spoke.'

'Yes,' said Tumnus. 'And when I supped with the Grand Vizier last night, it was the same. He asked me how I liked Tashbaan. And I (for I could not tell him I hated every stone of it and I would not lie) told him that now, when high summer was coming on, my heart turned to the cool woods and dewy slopes of Narnia. He gave a smile that meant no good and said, "There is nothing to hinder you from dancing there again, little goatfoot; *always provided you leave us in exchange a bride for our prince*."'

'Do you mean he would make me his wife by force?' exclaimed Susan.

'That's my fear, Susan,' said Edmund. 'Wife: or slave, which is worse.'

'But how can he? Does the Tisroc think our brother the High King would suffer such an outrage?'

'Sire,' said Peridan to the King. 'They would not be so mad. Do they think there are no swords and spears in Narnia?'

'Alas,' said Edmund. 'My guess is that the Tisroc has very small fear of Narnia. We are a little land. And little lands on the borders of a great empire were always hateful to the lords of the great empire. He longs to blot them out, gobble them up. When first he suffered the Prince to come to Cair Paravel as your lover, sister, it may be that he was only seeking an occasion against us. Most likely he hopes to make one mouthful of Narnia and Archenland both.'

'Let him try,' said the second Dwarf. 'At sea we are as big as he is. And if he assaults us by land, he has the desert to cross.'

'True, friend,' said Edmund. 'But is the desert a sure defence? What does Sallowpad say?'

'I know that desert well,' said the Raven. 'For I have flown above it far and wide in my younger days,' (you may be sure that Shasta pricked up his ears at this point).

'And this is certain; that if the Tisroc goes by the great oasis he can never lead a great army across it into Archenland. For though they could reach the oasis by the end of their first day's march, yet the springs there would be too little for the thirst of all those soldiers and their beasts. But there is another way.'

Shasta listened more attentively still.

'He that would find that way,' said the Raven, 'must start from the Tombs of the Ancient Kings and ride north-west so that the double peak of Mount Pire is always straight ahead of him. And so, in a day's riding or a little more, he shall come to the head of a stony valley, which is so narrow that a man might be within a furlong of it a thousand times and never know that it was there. And looking down this valley he will see neither grass nor water nor anything else good. But if he rides on down it he will come to a river and can ride by that water all the way into Archenland.'

'And do the Calormenes know of this Western way?' asked the Queen.

'Friends, friends,' said Edmund, 'what is the use of all this discourse? We are not asking whether Narnia or Calormen would win if war arose between them. We are asking how to save the honour of the Queen and our own lives out of this devilish city. For though my brother, Peter the High King, defeated the Tisroc a dozen times over, yet long before that day our throats would be cut and the Queen's grace would be the wife, or more likely, the slave, of this prince.'

'We have our weapons, King,' said the first Dwarf. 'And this is a reasonably defensible house.'

'As to that,' said the King, 'I do not doubt that every

one of us would sell our lives dearly in the gate and they would not come at the Queen but over our dead bodies. Yet we should be merely rats fighting in a trap when all's said.'

'Very true,' croaked the Raven. 'These last stands in a house make good stories, but nothing ever came of them. After their first few repulses the enemy always set the house on fire.'

'I am the cause of all this,' said Susan, bursting into tears. 'Oh, if only I had never left Cair Paravel. Our last happy day was before those ambassadors came from Calormen. The Moles were planting an orchard for us ... oh ... oh.' And she buried her face in her hands and sobbed.

'Courage, Su, courage,' said Edmund. 'Remember – but what is the matter with *you*, Master Tumnus?' For the Faun was holding both his horns with his hands as if he were trying to keep his head on by them and writhing to and fro as if he had a pain in his inside.

'Don't speak to me, don't speak to me,' said Tumnus. 'I'm thinking. I'm thinking so that I can hardly breathe. Wait, wait, do wait.'

There was a moment's puzzled silence and then the Faun looked up, drew a long breath, mopped its forehead and said:

'The only difficulty is how to get down to our ship – with some stores, too – without being seen and stopped.'

'Yes,' said a Dwarf dryly. 'Just as the beggar's only difficulty about riding is that he has no horse.'

'Wait, wait,' said Mr Tumnus impatiently. 'All we need is some pretext for going down to our ship today and taking stuff on board.'

'Yes,' said King Edmund doubtfully.

'Well, then,' said the Faun, 'how would it be if your Majesties bade the Prince to a great banquet to be held on board our own galleon, the *Splendour Hyaline*, tomorrow night? And let the message be worded as graciously as the Queen can contrive without pledging her honour: so as to give the Prince a hope that she is weakening.'

'This is very good counsel, Sire,' croaked the Raven.

'And then,' continued Tumnus excitedly, 'everyone will expect us to be going down to the ship all day, making preparations for our guests. And let some of us go to the bazaars and spend every minim we have at the fruiterers and the sweetmeat sellers and the wine merchants, just as we would if we were really giving a feast. And let us order magicians and jugglers and dancing girls and flute players, all to be on board tomorrow night.'

'I see, I see,' said King Edmund, rubbing his hands.

'And then,' said Tumnus, 'we'll all be on board tonight. And as soon as it is quite dark – '

'Up sails and out oars – !' said the King.

'And so to sea,' cried Tumnus, leaping up and beginning to dance.

'And our nose Northward,' said the first Dwarf.

'Running for home! Hurrah for Narnia and the North!' said the other.

'And the Prince waking next morning and finding his birds flown!' said Peridan, clapping his hands.

'Oh Master Tumnus, dear Master Tumnus,' said the Queen, catching his hands and swinging with him as he danced. 'You have saved us all.'

'The Prince will chase us,' said another lord, whose name Shasta had not heard.

'That's the least of my fears,' said Edmund. 'I have seen

all the shipping in the river and there's no tall ship of war nor swift galley there. I wish he may chase us! For the *Splendour Hyaline* could sink anything he has to send after her – if we were overtaken at all.'

'Sire,' said the Raven. 'You shall hear no better plot than the Faun's though we sat in council for seven days. And

now, as we birds say, nests before eggs. Which is as much as to say, let us all take our food and then at once be about our business.'

Everyone arose at this and the doors were opened and the lords and the creatures stood aside for the King and Queen to go out first. Shasta wondered what he ought to do, but Mr Tumnus said, 'Lie there, your Highness, and I will bring you up a little feast to yourself in a few moments. There is no need for you to move until we are all ready to embark.' Shasta laid his head down again on the pillows and soon he was alone in the room.

'This is perfectly dreadful,' thought Shasta. It never came into his head to tell these Narnians the whole truth and ask for their help. Having been brought up by a hard, close-fisted man like Arsheesh, he had a fixed habit of never telling grown-ups anything if he could help it: he thought they would always spoil or stop whatever you were trying to do. And he thought that even if the Narnian King might be friendly to the two horses, because they were Talking Beasts of Narnia, he would hate Aravis, because she was a Calormene, and either sell her for a slave or send her back to her father. As for himself, 'I simply daren't tell them I'm not Prince Corin *now*,' thought Shasta. 'I've heard all their plans. If they knew I wasn't one of themselves, they'd never let me out of this house alive. They'd be afraid I'd betray them to the Tisroc. They'd kill me. And if the real Corin turns up, it'll all come out, and they *will*!' He had, you see, no idea of how noble and free-born people behave.

'What am I to do? What am I to do?' he kept saying to himself. 'What – hullo, here comes that goaty little creature again.'

The Faun trotted in, half dancing, with a tray in its hands which was nearly as large as itself. This he set on an inlaid table beside Shasta's sofa, and sat down himself on the carpeted floor with his goaty legs crossed.

'Now, princeling,' he said. 'Make a good dinner. It will be your last meal in Tashbaan.'

It was a fine meal after the Calormene fashion. I don't know whether you would have liked it or not, but Shasta did. There were lobsters, and salad, and snipe stuffed with almonds and truffles, and a complicated dish made of chicken-livers and rice and raisins and nuts, and there were cool melons and gooseberry fools and mulberry fools, and every kind of nice thing that can be made with ice. There was also a little flagon of the sort of wine that is called 'white' though it is really yellow.

While Shasta was eating, the good little Faun, who thought he was still dazed with sunstroke, kept talking to him about the fine times he would have when they all got home; about his good old father King Lune of Archenland and the little castle where he lived on the southern

slopes of the pass. 'And don't forget,' said Mr Tumnus, 'that you are promised your first suit of armour and your first war horse on your next birthday. And then your Highness will begin to learn how to tilt and joust. And in a few years, if all goes well, King Peter has promised your royal father that he himself will make you Knight at Cair Paravel. And in the meantime there will be plenty of comings and goings between Narnia and Archenland across the neck of the mountains. And of course you remember you have promised to come for a whole week to stay with me for the Summer Festival, and there'll be bonfires and all-night dances of Fauns and Dryads in the heart of the woods and, who knows? – we might see Aslan himself!'

When the meal was over the Faun told Shasta to stay quietly where he was. 'And it wouldn't do you any harm to have a little sleep,' he added. 'I'll call you in plenty of time to get on board. And then, Home. Narnia and the North!'

Shasta had so enjoyed his dinner and all the things Tumnus had been telling him that when he was left alone his thoughts took a different turn. He only hoped now that the real Prince Corin would not turn up until it was too late and that he would be taken away to Narnia by ship. I am afraid he did not think at all of what might happen to the real Corin when he was left behind in Tashbaan. He was a little worried about Aravis and Bree waiting for him at the Tombs. But then he said to himself, 'Well, how can I help it?' and, 'Anyway, that Aravis thinks she's too good to go about with me, so she can jolly well go alone,' and at the same time he couldn't help feeling that it would be much nicer going to Narnia by sea than toiling across the desert.

When he had thought all this he did what I expect you would have done if you had been up very early and had a long walk and a great deal of excitement and then a very good meal, and were lying on a sofa in a cool room with no noise in it except when a bee came buzzing in through the wide open windows. He fell asleep.

What woke him was a loud crash. He jumped up off the sofa, staring. He saw at once from the mere look of the room – the lights and shadows all looked different – that he must have slept for several hours. He saw also what had made the crash: a costly porcelain vase which had been standing on the window-sill lay on the floor broken into about thirty pieces. But he hardly noticed all these things. What he did notice was two hands gripping the window-sill from outside. They gripped harder and harder (getting white at the knuckles) and then up came a head and a pair of shoulders. A moment later there was a boy of Shasta's own age sitting astride of the sill with one leg hanging down inside the room.

Shasta had never seen his own face in a looking-glass. Even if he had, he might not have realized that the other boy was (at ordinary times) almost exactly like himself. At the moment this boy was not particularly like anyone for

he had the finest black eye you ever saw, and a tooth missing, and his clothes (which must have been splendid ones when he put them on) were torn and dirty, and there was both blood and mud on his face.

'Who are you?' said the boy in a whisper.

'Are you Prince Corin?' said Shasta.

'Yes, of course,' said the other. 'But who are you?'

'I'm nobody, nobody in particular, I mean,' said Shasta. 'King Edmund caught me in the street and mistook me for you. I suppose we must look like one another. Can I get out the way you've got in?'

'Yes, if you're any good at climbing,' said Corin. 'But

why are you in such a hurry? I say: we ought to be able to get some fun out of this being mistaken for one another.'

'No, no,' said Shasta. 'We must change places at once. It'll be simply frightful if Mr Tumnus comes back and finds us both here. I've had to pretend to be you. And you're starting tonight – secretly. And where were you all this time?'

'A boy in the street made a beastly joke about Queen Susan,' said Prince Corin, 'so I knocked him down. He ran howling into a house and his big brother came out. So I knocked the big brother down. Then they all followed me until we ran into three old men with spears who are called the Watch. So I fought with the Watch and they knocked me down. It was getting dark by now. Then the Watch took me along to lock me up somewhere. So I asked them if they'd like a stoup of wine and they said they didn't mind if they did. Then I took them to a wine shop and got them some and they all sat down and drank till they fell asleep. I thought it was time for me to be off so I came out quietly and then I found the first boy – the one who had started all the trouble – still hanging about. So I knocked him down again. After that I climbed up a pipe on to the roof of a house and lay quiet till it began to get light this morning. Ever since that I've been finding my way back. I say, is there anything to drink?'

'No, I drank it,' said Shasta. 'And now, show me how you got in. There's not a minute to lose. You'd better lie down on the sofa and pretend – but I forgot. It'll be no good with all those bruises and black eye. You'll just have to tell them the truth, once I'm safely away.'

'What else did you think I'd be telling them?' asked the Prince with a rather angry look. 'And who are *you*?'

'There's no time,' said Shasta in a frantic whisper. 'I'm a Narnian, I believe; something Northern anyway. But I've been brought up all my life in Calormen. And I'm escaping: across the desert; with a talking Horse called Bree. And now, quick! How do I get away?'

'Look,' said Corin. 'Drop from this window on to the roof of the verandah. But you must do it lightly, on your toes, or someone will hear you. Then along to your left and you can get up to the top of that wall if you're any good at all as a climber. Then along the wall to the corner. Drop onto the rubbish heap you will find outside, and there you are.'

'Thanks,' said Shasta, who was already sitting on the sill. The two boys were looking into each other's faces and suddenly found that they were friends.

'Good-bye,' said Corin. 'And *good* luck. I do hope you get safe away.'

'Good-bye,' said Shasta. 'I say, you have been having some adventures!'

'Nothing to yours,' said the Prince. 'Now drop; lightly – I say,' he added as Shasta dropped, 'I hope we meet in Archenland. Go to my father King Lune and tell him you're a friend of mine. Look out! I hear someone coming.'

CHAPTER 6

SHASTA AMONG THE TOMBS

SHASTA ran lightly along the roof on tiptoes. It felt hot to his bare feet. He was only a few seconds scrambling up the wall at the far end and when he got to the corner he found himself looking down into a narrow, smelly street, and there was a rubbish heap against the outside of the wall just as Corin had told him. Before jumping down he took a rapid glance round him to get his bearings. Apparently he had now come over the crown of the island-hill on which Tashbaan is built. Everything sloped away before him, flat roofs below flat roofs, down to the towers and battlements of the city's Northern wall. Beyond that was the river and beyond the river a short slope covered with gardens. But beyond that again there was something he had never seen the like of – a great yellowish-grey thing, flat as a calm sea, and stretching for miles. On the far side of it were huge blue things, lumpy but with jagged edges, and some of them with white tops. 'The desert! the mountains!' thought Shasta.

He jumped down on to the rubbish and began trotting along downhill as fast as he could in the narrow lane, which soon brought him into a wider street where there were more people. No one bothered to look at a little ragged boy running along on bare feet. Still, he was anxious and uneasy till he turned a corner and there saw the city gate in front of him. Here he was pressed and jostled a bit, for a good many other people were also going out; and on the bridge beyond the gate the crowd became quite a slow procession, more like a queue than a crowd. Out there, with clear running water on each side, it was deliciously fresh after the smell and heat and noise of Tashbaan.

When once Shasta had reached the far end of the bridge he found the crowd melting away; everyone seemed to be going either to the left or right along the river bank. He went straight ahead up a road that did not appear to be much used, between gardens. In a few paces he was alone, and a few more brought him to the top of the slope. There he stood and stared. It was like coming to the end of the world for all the grass stopped quite suddenly a few feet before him and the sand began: endless level sand like on a sea shore but a bit rougher because it was never wet. The mountains, which now looked further off than before, loomed ahead. Greatly to his relief he saw, about five minutes' walk away on his left, what must certainly be the Tombs, just as Bree had described them; great masses of mouldering stone shaped like gigantic bee-hives, but a little narrower. They looked very black and grim, for the sun was now setting right behind them.

He turned his face West and trotted towards the Tombs. He could not help looking out very hard for any sign of his friends, though the setting sun shone in his face so that he could see hardly anything. 'And anyway,' he thought, 'of course they'll be round on the far side of the farthest Tomb, not this side where anyone might see them from the city.'

There were about twelve Tombs, each with a low arched doorway that opened into absolute blackness. They were dotted about in no kind of order, so that it took a long time, going round this one and going round that one, before you could be sure that you had looked round every side of every tomb. This was what Shasta had to do. There was nobody there.

It was very quiet here out on the edge of the desert; and now the sun had really set.

Suddenly from somewhere behind him there came a terrible sound. Shasta's heart gave a great jump and he had to bite his tongue to keep himself from screaming. Next moment he realized what it was: the horns of Tashbaan blowing for the closing of the gates. 'Don't be a silly little coward,' said Shasta to himself. 'Why, it's only the same noise you heard this morning.' But there is a great difference between a noise heard letting you in with your friends in the morning, and a noise heard alone at nightfall, shutting you out. And now that the gates were shut he knew there was no chance of the others joining him that evening. 'Either they're shut up in Tashbaan for the night,'

thought Shasta, 'or else they've gone on without me. It's just the sort of thing that Aravis would do. But Bree wouldn't. Oh, he wouldn't – now, would he?'

In this idea about Aravis Shasta was once more quite wrong. She was proud and could be hard enough but she was as true as steel and would never have deserted a companion, whether she liked him or not.

Now that Shasta knew he would have to spend the night alone (it was getting darker every minute) he began to like the look of the place less and less. There was something very uncomfortable about those great, silent shapes of stone. He had been trying his hardest for a long time not to think of ghouls: but he couldn't keep it up any longer.

'Ow! Ow! Help!' he shouted suddenly, for at that very moment he felt something touch his leg. I don't think anyone can be blamed for shouting if something comes up from behind and touches him; not in such a place and at such a time, when he is frightened already. Shasta at any rate was too frightened to run. Anything would be better than being chased round and round the burial places of the Ancient Kings with something he dared not look at behind him. Instead, he did what was really the most sensible thing he could do. He looked round; and his heart almost burst with relief. What had touched him was only a cat.

The light was too bad now for Shasta to see much of the cat except that it was big and very solemn. It looked as if it might have lived for long, long years among the Tombs, alone. Its eyes made you think it knew secrets it would not tell.

'Puss, puss,' said Shasta. 'I suppose you're not a *talking* cat.'

The cat stared at him harder than ever. Then it started walking away, and of course Shasta followed it. It led him right through the Tombs and out on the desert side of them. There it sat down bolt upright with its tail curled round its feet and its face set towards the desert and towards Narnia and the North, as still as if it were watching for some enemy. Shasta lay down beside it with his back against the cat and his face towards the Tombs, because if one is nervous there's nothing like having your face towards the danger and having something warm and solid at your back. The sand wouldn't have seemed very comfortable to you, but Shasta had been sleeping on the ground for weeks and hardly noticed it. Very soon he fell asleep, though even in his dreams he went on wondering what had happened to Bree and Aravis and Hwin.

He was wakened suddenly by a noise he had never heard before. 'Perhaps it was only a nightmare,' said Shasta to himself. At the same moment he noticed that the cat had gone from his back, and he wished it hadn't. But he lay quite still without even opening his eyes because he felt sure he would be more frightened if he sat up and looked round at the Tombs and the loneliness: just as you or I might lie still with the clothes over our heads. But then the noise came again – a harsh, piercing cry from behind him out of the desert. Then of course he had to open his eyes and sit up.

The moon was shining brightly. The Tombs – far bigger and nearer than he had thought they would be – looked grey in the moonlight. In fact, they looked horribly like huge people, draped in grey robes that covered their heads and faces. They were not at all nice things to have near you when spending a night alone in a strange place. But the noise had come from the opposite side, from the desert. Shasta had to turn his back on the Tombs (he didn't like that much) and stare out across the level sand. The wild cry rang out again.

'I hope it's not more lions,' thought Shasta. It was in fact not very like the lion's roars he had heard on the night when they met Hwin and Aravis, and was really the cry of a jackal. But of course Shasta did not know this. Even if he had known, he would not have wanted very much to meet a jackal.

The cries rang out again and again. 'There's more than one of them, whatever they are,' thought Shasta. 'And they're coming nearer.'

I suppose that if he had been an entirely sensible boy he would have gone back through the Tombs nearer to the river where there were houses, and wild beasts would be less likely to come. But then there were (or he thought there were) the ghouls. To go back through the Tombs would mean going past those dark openings in the Tombs; and what might come out of them? It may have been silly, but Shasta felt he had rather risk the wild beasts. Then, as the cries came nearer and nearer, he began to change his mind.

He was just going to run for it when suddenly, between him and the desert, a huge animal bounded into view. As the moon was behind it, it looked quite black, and Shasta did not know what it was, except that it had a very big, shaggy head and went on four legs. It did not seem to have noticed Shasta, for it suddenly stopped, turned its head towards the desert and let out a roar which re-echoed through the Tombs and seemed to shake the sand under Shasta's feet. The cries of the other creatures suddenly

stopped and he thought he could hear feet scampering
away. Then the great beast turned to examine Shasta.

'It's a lion, I know it's a lion,' thought Shasta. 'I'm done.
I wonder will it hurt much. I wish it was over. I wonder
does anything happen to people after they're dead. O-o-oh!
Here it comes!' And he shut his eyes and his teeth tight.

But instead of teeth and claws he only felt something
warm lying down at his feet. And when he opened his eyes
he said, 'Why, it's not nearly as big as I thought! It's only
half the size. No, it isn't even quarter the size. I do declare
it's only the cat!! I must have dreamed all that about its
being as big as a horse.'

And whether he really had been dreaming or no, what
was now lying at his feet, and staring him out of countenance with its big, green, unwinking eyes, was the cat;
though certainly one of the largest cats he had ever seen.

'Oh, Puss,' gasped Shasta. 'I *am* so glad to see you again.
I've been having such horrible dreams.' And he at once
lay down again, back to back with the cat as they had been
at the beginning of the night. The warmth from it spread
all over him.

'I'll never do anything nasty to a cat again as long as I
live,' said Shasta, half to the cat and half to himself. 'I did
once, you know. I threw stones at a half-starved mangy old
stray. Hey! Stop that.' For the cat had turned round and
given him a scratch. 'None of that,' said Shasta. 'It isn't as
if you could understand what I'm saying.' Then he dozed
off.

Next morning when he woke, the cat was gone, the sun
was already up, and the sand hot. Shasta, very thirsty, sat
up and rubbed his eyes. The desert was blindingly white
and, though there was a murmur of noises from the city

behind him, where he sat everything was perfectly still. When he looked a little left and west, so that the sun was not in his eyes, he could see the mountains on the far side of the desert, so sharp and clear that they looked only a stone's throw away. He particularly noticed one blue height that divided into two peaks at the top and decided that it must be Mount Pire. 'That's our direction, judging by what the Raven said,' he thought, 'so I'll just make sure of it, so as not to waste any time when the others turn up.' So he made a good, deep straight furrow with his foot pointing exactly to Mount Pire.

The next job, clearly, was to get something to eat and drink. Shasta trotted back through the Tombs – they looked quite ordinary now and he wondered how he could ever have been afraid of them – and down into the cultivated land by the river's side. There were a few people about but not very many, for the city gates had been open several hours and the early morning crowds had already gone in. So he had no difficulty in doing a little 'raiding' (as Bree called it). It involved a climb over a garden wall and the results were three oranges, a melon, a fig or two, and a pomegranate. After that, he went down to the river bank, but not too near the bridge, and had a drink. The water was so nice that he took off his hot, dirty clothes and had a dip; for of course Shasta, having lived on the shore all his life, had learned to swim almost as soon as he had learned to walk. When he came out he lay on the grass looking across the water at Tashbaan – all the splendour and strength and glory of it. But that made him remember the dangers of it too. He suddenly realized that the others might have reached the Tombs while he was bathing ('and gone on without me, as likely as not'), so he dressed in a fright and tore back at such a speed that he was all hot and thirsty when he arrived and so the good of his bathe was gone.

Like most days when you are alone and waiting for something this day seemed about a hundred hours long. He had plenty to think of, of course, but sitting alone, just thinking, is pretty slow. He thought a good deal about the Narnians and especially about Corin. He wondered what had happened when they discovered that the boy who had been lying on the sofa and hearing all their secret plans wasn't really Corin at all. It was very unpleasant to think of all those nice people imagining him a traitor.

But as the sun slowly, slowly climbed up to the top of the sky and then slowly, slowly began going downwards to the West, and no one came and nothing at all happened, he began to get more and more anxious. And of course he now realized that when they arranged to wait for one another at the Tombs no one had said anything about How Long. He couldn't wait here for the rest of his life! And soon it would be dark again, and he would have another night just like last night. A dozen different plans went through his head, all wretched ones, and at last he fixed on the worst plan of all. He decided to wait till it was dark and then go back to the river and steal as many melons as he could carry and set out for Mount Pire alone, trusting for his direction to the line he had drawn that morning in the sand. It was a crazy idea and if he had read as many books as you have about journeys over deserts he would never have dreamed of it. But Shasta had read no books at all.

But before the sun set something did happen. Shasta was sitting in the shadow of one of the Tombs when he looked up and saw two horses coming towards him. Then his heart gave a great leap, for he recognized them as Bree and Hwin. But next moment his heart went down into his toes again. There was no sign of Aravis. The Horses were being led by a strange man, an armed man pretty handsomely dressed like an upper slave in a great family. Bree and Hwin were no longer got up like pack-horses, but saddled and bridled. And what could it all mean? 'It's a trap,' thought Shasta. 'Somebody has caught Aravis and perhaps they've tortured her and she's given the whole thing away. They want me to jump out and run up and speak to Bree and then I'll be caught too! And yet if I don't, I may be losing my only chance to meet the others. Oh I do wish I knew what had happened.' And he skulked behind the Tomb, looking out every few minutes, and wondering which was the least dangerous thing to do.

CHAPTER 7

ARAVIS IN TASHBAAN

WHAT had really happened was this. When Aravis saw Shasta hurried away by the Narnians and found herself alone with two horses who (very wisely) wouldn't say a word, she never lost her head even for a moment. She grabbed Bree's halter and stood still, holding both the horses; and though her heart was beating as hard as a hammer, she did nothing to show it. As soon as the Narnian lords had passed she tried to move on again. But before she could take a step, another crier ('Bother all these people' thought Aravis) was heard shouting out, 'Way, way, way! Way for the Tarkheena Lasaraleen!' and immediately, following the crier, came four armed slaves and then four bearers carrying a litter which was all a-flutter with silken curtains and all a-jingle with silver bells and which scented the whole street with perfumes and flowers. After the litter, female slaves in beautiful clothes, and then a few grooms, runners, pages, and the like. And now Aravis made her first mistake.

She knew Lasaraleen quite well – almost as if they had been at school together – because they had often stayed in the same houses and been to the same parties. And Aravis couldn't help looking up to see what Lasaraleen looked like now that she was married and a very great person indeed.

It was fatal. The eyes of the two girls met. And immediately Lasaraleen sat up in the litter and burst out at the top of her voice.

'Aravis! What on earth are you doing here? Your
father –'

There was not a moment to lose. Without a second's
delay Aravis let go the Horses, caught the edge of the litter,
swung herself up beside Lasaraleen and whispered furiously in her ear.

'Shut up! Do you hear! Shut up. You must hide me.
Tell your people –'

'But darling –' began Lasaraleen in the same loud voice.
(She didn't in the least mind making people stare; in fact
she rather liked it.)

'Do what I tell you or I'll never speak to you again,' hissed Aravis. 'Please, please be quick, Las. It's frightfully important. Tell your people to bring those two horses along. Pull all the curtains of the litter and get away somewhere where I can't be found. And do *hurry*.'

'All right, darling,' said Lasaraleen in her lazy voice. 'Here. Two of you take the Tarkheena's horses.' (This was to the slaves.) 'And now home. I say, darling, do you think we really want the curtains drawn on a day like this? I mean to say –'

But Aravis had already drawn the curtains, enclosing Lasaraleen and herself in a rich and scented, but rather stuffy, kind of tent.

'I mustn't be seen,' she said. 'My father doesn't know I'm here. I'm running away.'

'My dear, how perfectly thrilling,' said Lasaraleen. 'I'm dying to hear all about it. Darling, you're sitting on my dress. Do you mind? That's better. It is a new one. Do you like it? I got it at –'

'Oh, Las, do be serious,' said Aravis. 'Where is my father?'

'Didn't you know?' said Lasaraleen. 'He's here, of course. He came to town yesterday and is asking about you everywhere. And to think of you and me being here together and his not knowing anything about it! It's the funniest thing I ever heard.' And she went off into giggles. She always had been a terrible giggler, as Aravis now remembered.

'It isn't funny at all,' she said. 'It's dreadfully serious. Where can you hide me?'

'No difficulty at all, my dear girl,' said Lasaraleen. 'I'll take you home. My husband's away and no one will see you. Phew! It's not much fun with the curtains drawn. I want to see people. There's no point in having a new dress on if one's to go about shut up like this.'

'I hope no one heard you when you shouted out to me like that,' said Aravis.

'No, no, of course, darling,' said Lasaraleen absent-mindedly. 'But you haven't even told me yet what you think of the dress.'

'Another thing,' said Aravis. 'You must tell your people to treat those two horses very respectfully. That's part of the secret. They're really Talking Horses from Narnia.'

'Fancy!' said Lasaraleen. 'How exciting! And oh, darling, have you seen the barbarian queen from Narnia? She's staying in Tashbaan at present. They say Prince Rabadash is madly in love with her. There have been the most wonderful parties and hunts and things all this last fortnight. I can't see that she's so very pretty myself. But some of the Narnian *men* are lovely. I was taken out on a river party the day before yesterday, and I was wearing my –'

'How shall we prevent your people telling everyone that you've got a visitor – dressed like a beggar's brat – in your house? It might so easily get round to my father.'

'Now don't keep on fussing, there's a dear,' said Lasaraleen. 'We'll get you some proper clothes in a moment. And here we are!'

The bearers had stopped and the litter was being lowered. When the curtains had been drawn Aravis found that she was in a courtyard-garden very like the one that Shasta had been taken into a few minutes earlier in another part of the city. Lasaraleen would have gone indoors at once but Aravis reminded her in a frantic whisper to say something to the slaves about not telling anyone of their mistress's strange visitor.

'Sorry, darling, it had gone right out of my head,' said Lasaraleen. 'Here. All of you. And you, doorkeeper. No one is to be let out of the house today. And anyone I catch talking about this young lady will be first beaten to death and then burned alive and after that be kept on bread and water for six weeks. There.'

Although Lasaraleen had said she was dying to hear Aravis's story, she showed no sign of really wanting to hear it at all. She was, in fact, much better at talking than at listening. She insisted on Aravis having a long and luxurious bath (Calormene baths are famous) and then dressing her up in the finest clothes before she would let her explain anything. The fuss she made about choosing the dresses nearly drove Aravis mad. She remembered now that Lasaraleen had always been like that, interested in clothes and parties and gossip. Aravis had always been more interested in bows and arrows and horses and dogs and swimming. You will guess that each thought the other silly. But when at last they were both seated after a meal (it was chiefly of the whipped cream and jelly and fruit and ice sort) in a beautiful pillared room (which Aravis would have liked better if Lasaraleen's spoiled pet monkey hadn't been climbing about it all the time) Lasaraleen at last asked her why she was running away from home.

When Aravis had finished telling her story, Lasaraleen said, 'But, darling, why *don't* you marry Ahoshta Tarkaan? Everyone's crazy about him. My husband says he is beginning to be one of the greatest men in Calormen. He has just been made Grand Vizier now old Axartha has died. Didn't you know?'

'I don't care. I can't stand the sight of him,' said Aravis.

'But, darling, only think! Three palaces, and one of them that beautiful one down on the lake at Ilkeen. Positively ropes of pearls, I'm told. Baths of asses' milk. And you'd see such a lot of *me*.'

'He can keep his pearls and palaces as far as I'm concerned,' said Aravis.

'You always *were* a queer girl, Aravis,' said Lasaraleen. 'What more *do* you want?'

In the end, however, Aravis managed to make her friend believe that she was in earnest and even to discuss plans. There would be no difficulty now about getting the two horses out of the North gate and then on to the Tombs. No one would stop or question a groom in fine clothes leading a war horse and a lady's saddle horse down to the river, and Lasaraleen had plenty of grooms to send. It wasn't so easy to decide what to do about Aravis herself. She suggested that she could be carried out in the litter with the curtains drawn. But Lasaraleen told her that litters were only used in the city and the sight of one going out through the gate would be certain to lead to questions.

When they had talked for a long time – and it was all the longer because Aravis found it hard to keep her friend to the point – at last Lasaraleen clapped her hands and said, 'Oh, I have an idea. There is *one* way of getting out of the city without using the gates. The Tisroc's garden (may he live for ever!) runs right down to the water and there is a little water-door. Only for the palace people of course – but then you know, dear (here she tittered a little) we almost *are* palace people. I say, it is lucky for you that you came to *me*. The dear Tisroc (may he live for ever!) is *so* kind. We're asked to the palace almost every day and it is like a second home. I love all the dear princes and princesses and I positively *adore* Prince Rabadash. I might run in and see any of the palace ladies at any hour of the day or night. Why shouldn't I slip in with you, after dark, and let you out by the water-door? There are always a few punts and things tied up outside it. And even if we were caught—'

'All would be lost,' said Aravis.

'Oh darling, don't get so excited,' said Lasaraleen. 'I was going to say, even if we were caught everyone would only say it was one of my mad jokes. I'm getting quite well known for them. Only the other day – do listen, dear, this is frightfully funny—'

'I meant, all would be lost *for me*,' said Aravis a little sharply.

'Oh – ah – yes – I *do* see what you mean, darling. Well, can you think of any better plan?'

Aravis couldn't, and answered, 'No. We'll have to risk it. When can we start?'

'Oh, not tonight,' said Lasaraleen. 'Of course not tonight. There's a great feast on tonight (I must start getting my hair done for it in a few minutes) and the whole place will be a blaze of lights. And such a crowd too! It would have to be tomorrow night.'

This was bad news for Aravis, but she had to make the best of it. The afternoon passed very slowly and it was a relief when Lasaraleen went out to the banquet, for Aravis was very tired of her giggling and her talk about dresses and parties, weddings and engagements and scandals. She went to bed early and that part she did enjoy: it was so nice to have pillows and sheets again.

But the next day passed very slowly. Lasaraleen wanted to go back on the whole arrangement and kept on telling Aravis that Narnia was a country of perpetual snow and ice inhabited by demons and sorcerers, and she was mad to think of going there. 'And with a peasant boy, too!' said Lasaraleen. 'Darling, think of it! It's not Nice.' Aravis had thought of it a good deal, but she was so tired of Lasaraleen's silliness by now that, for the first time, she began to think that travelling with Shasta was really rather more fun than fashionable life in Tashbaan. So she only replied, 'You forget that I'll be a nobody, just like him, when we get to Narnia. And anyway, I promised.'

'And to think,' said Lasaraleen, almost crying, 'that if only you had sense you could be the wife of a Grand Vizier!' Aravis went away to have a private word with the horses.

'You must go with a groom a little before sunset down to the Tombs,' she said. 'No more of those packs. You'll be saddled and bridled again. But there'll have to be food in Hwin's saddle-bags and a full water-skin behind yours, Bree. The man has orders to let you both have a good long drink at the far side of the bridge.'

'And then, Narnia and the North!' whispered Bree. 'But what if Shasta is not at the Tombs?'

'Wait for him of course,' said Aravis. 'I hope you've been quite comfortable.'

'Never better stabled in my life,' said Bree. 'But if the husband of that tittering Tarkheena friend of yours is paying his head groom to get the best oats, then I think the head groom is cheating him.'

Aravis and Lasaraleen had supper in the pillared room.

About two hours later they were ready to start. Aravis was dressed to look like a superior slave-girl in a great house and wore a veil over her face. They had agreed that if any questions were asked Lasaraleen would pretend that Aravis was a slave she was taking as a present to one of the princesses.

The two girls went out on foot. A very few minutes brought them to the palace gates. Here there were of course soldiers on guard but the officer knew Lasaraleen quite well and called his men to attention and saluted. They passed at once into the Hall of Black Marble. A fair number of courtiers, slaves and others were still moving about here but this only made the two girls less conspicuous. They passed on into the Hall of Pillars and then into the Hall of Statues and down the colonnade, passing the great beaten-copper doors of the throne room.

It was all magnificent beyond description; what they could see of it in the dim light of the lamps.

Presently they came out into the garden-court which sloped downhill in a number of terraces. On the far side of that they came to the Old Palace. It had already grown almost quite dark and they now found themselves in a maze of corridors lit only by occasional torches fixed in brackets to the walls. Lasaraleen halted at a place where you had to go either left or right.

'Go on, do go on,' whispered Aravis, whose heart was beating terribly and who still felt that her father might run into them at any corner.

'I'm just wondering . . .' said Lasaraleen. 'I'm not absolutely sure which way we go from here. I *think* it's the left. Yes, I'm almost sure it's the left. What fun this is!'

They took the left hand way and found themselves in a passage that was hardly lighted at all and which soon began going down steps.

'It's all right,' said Lasaraleen. 'I'm sure we're right now. I remember these steps.' But at that moment a moving light appeared ahead. A second later there appeared from round a distant corner, the dark shapes of two men walking backwards and carrying tall candles. And of course it is only before royalties that people walk backwards. Aravis felt Lasaraleen grip her arm – that sort of sudden grip which is almost a pinch and which means that the person who is gripping you is very frightened indeed. Aravis thought it odd that Lasaraleen should be so afraid of the Tisroc if he were really such a friend of hers, but there was no time to go on thinking. Lasaraleen was hurrying her back to the top of the steps, on tiptoe, and groping wildly along the wall.

'Here's a door,' she whispered. 'Quick.'

They went in, drew the door very softly behind them, and found themselves in pitch darkness. Aravis could hear by Lasaraleen's breathing that she was terrified.

'Tash preserve us!' whispered Lasaraleen. 'What *shall* we do if he comes in here. Can we hide?'

There was a soft carpet under their feet. They groped forward into the room and blundered on to a sofa.

'Let's lie down behind it,' whimpered Lasaraleen. 'Oh, I *do* wish we hadn't come.'

There was just room between the sofa and the curtained wall and the two girls got down. Lasaraleen managed to get the better position and was completely covered. The upper part of Aravis's face stuck out beyond the sofa, so that if anyone came into that room with a light and happened to look in exactly the right place they would see her. But of course, because she was wearing a veil, what they saw would not at once look like a forehead and a pair of eyes. Aravis shoved desperately to try to make Lasaraleen give her a little more room. But Lasaraleen, now quite selfish in her panic, fought back and pinched her feet. They gave it up and lay still, panting a little. Their own breath seemed dreadfully noisy, but there was no other noise.

'Is it safe?' said Aravis at last in the tiniest possible whisper.

'I – I – *think* so,' began Lasaraleen. 'But my poor nerves—' and then came the most terrible noise they could have heard at that moment: the noise of the door opening. And then came light. And because Aravis couldn't get her head any further in behind the sofa, she saw everything.

First came the two slaves (deaf and dumb, as Aravis

rightly guessed, and therefore used at the most secret councils) walking backwards and carrying the candles. They took up their stand one at each end of the sofa. This was a good thing, for of course it was now harder for anyone to see Aravis once a slave was in front of her and she was looking between his heels. Then came an old man, very fat, wearing a curious pointed cap by which she immediately knew that he was the Tisroc. The least of the jewels with which he was covered was worth more than all the clothes and weapons of the Narnian lords put together: but he was so fat and such a mass of frills and pleats and bobbles and buttons and tassels and talismans that Aravis couldn't help thinking the Narnian fashions (at any rate for men) looked nicer. After him came a tall young man with a feathered and jewelled turban on his head and an ivory-sheathed scimitar at his side. He seemed very excited and his eyes and teeth flashed fiercely in the candlelight. Last of all came a little hump-backed, wizened old man in whom she recognized with a shudder the new Grand Vizier and her own betrothed husband, Ahoshta Tarkaan himself.

As soon as all three had entered the room and the door was shut, the Tisroc seated himself on the divan with a sigh of contentment, the young man took his place, standing before him, and the Grand Vizier got down on his knees and elbows and laid his face flat on the carpet.

CHAPTER 8

IN THE HOUSE OF THE TISROC

'Oh-my-father-and-oh-the-delight-of-my-eyes,' began the young man, muttering the words very quickly and sulkily and not at all as if the Tisroc *were* the delight of his eyes. 'May you live for ever, but you have utterly destroyed me. If you had given me the swiftest of the galleys at sunrise when I first saw that the ship of the accursed barbarians was gone from her place I would perhaps have overtaken them. But you persuaded me to send first and see if they had not merely moved round the point into better anchorage. And now the whole day has been wasted. And they are gone – gone – out of my reach! The false jade, the—' and here he added a great many descriptions of Queen Susan which would not look at all nice in print. For of course this young man was Prince Rabadash and of course the false jade was Susan of Narnia.

'Compose yourself, O my son,' said the Tisroc. 'For the departure of guests makes a wound that is easily healed in the heart of a judicious host.'

'But I *want* her,' cried the Prince. 'I must have her. I shall die if I do not get her – false, proud, black-hearted daughter of a dog that she is! I cannot sleep and my food has no savour and my eyes are darkened because of her beauty. I must have the barbarian queen.'

'How well it was said by a gifted poet,' observed the Vizier, raising his face (in a somewhat dusty condition) from the carpet, 'that deep draughts from the fountain of reason are desirable in order to extinguish the fire of youthful love.'

This seemed to exasperate the Prince. 'Dog,' he shouted, directing a series of well-aimed kicks at the hindquarters of the Vizier, 'do not dare to quote the poets to me. I have had maxims and verses flung at me all day and I can endure

them no more.' I am afraid Aravis did not feel at all sorry for the Vizier.

The Tisroc was apparently sunk in thought, but when, after a long pause, he noticed what was happening, he said tranquilly:

'My son, by all means desist from kicking the venerable and enlightened Vizier: for as a costly jewel retains its value even if hidden in a dung-hill, so old age and dis-cretion are to be respected even in the vile persons of our subjects. Desist therefore, and tell us what you desire and propose.'

'I desire and propose, O my father,' said Rabadash, 'that you immediately call out your invincible armies and invade the thrice-accursed land of Narnia and waste it with fire and sword and add it to your illimitable empire, killing their High King and all of his blood except the Queen Susan. For I must have her as my wife, though she shall learn a sharp lesson first.'

'Understand, O my son,' said the Tisroc, 'that no words you can speak will move me to an open war against Narnia.'

'If you were not my father, O ever-living Tisroc,' said the Prince, grinding his teeth, 'I should say that was the word of a coward.'

'And if you were not my son, O most inflammable Rabadash,' replied his father, 'your life would be short and your death slow when you had said it.' (The cool, placid voice in which he spoke these words made Aravis's blood run cold.)

'But why, O my father,' said the Prince – this time in a much more respectful voice, 'why should we think twice about punishing Narnia any more than about hanging an idle slave or sending a worn-out horse to be made into dog's-meat? It is not the fourth size of one of your least provinces. A thousand spears could conquer it in five weeks. It is an unseemly blot on the skirts of your empire.'

'Most undoubtedly,' said the Tisroc. 'These little barbarian countries that call themselves *free* (which is as much as to say, idle, disordered, and unprofitable) are hateful to the gods and to all persons of discernment.'

'Then why have we suffered such a land as Narnia to remain thus long unsubdued?'

'Know, O enlightened Prince,' said the Grand Vizier, 'that until the year in which your exalted father began his salutary and unending reign, the land of Narnia was covered with ice and snow and was moreover ruled by a most powerful enchantress.'

'This I know very well, O loquacious Vizier,' answered the Prince. 'But I know also that the enchantress is dead. And the ice and snow have vanished, so that Narnia is now wholesome, fruitful, and delicious.'

'And this change, O most learned Prince, has doubtless been brought to pass by the powerful incantations of those wicked persons who now call themselves kings and queens of Narnia.'

'I am rather of the opinion,' said Rabadash, 'that it has come about by the alteration of the stars and the operation of natural causes.'

'All this,' said the Tisroc, 'is a question for the disputations of learned men. I will never believe that so great an alteration, and the killing of the old enchantress, were effected without the aid of strong magic. And such things are to be expected in that land, which is chiefly inhabited by demons in the shape of beasts that talk like men, and monsters that are half man and half beast. It is commonly reported that the High King of Narnia (whom may the gods utterly reject) is supported by a demon of hideous aspect and irresistible maleficence who appears in the shape of a Lion. Therefore the attacking of Narnia is a dark and doubtful enterprise, and I am determined not to put my hand out farther than I can draw it back.'

'How blessed is Calormen,' said the Vizier, popping up his face again, 'on whose ruler the gods have been pleased to bestow prudence and circumspection! Yet as the irrefutable and sapient Tisroc has said it is very grievous to be constrained to keep our hands off such a dainty dish as Narnia. Gifted was that poet who said—' but at this point

Ahoshta noticed an impatient movement of the Prince's toe and became suddenly silent.

'It is very grievous,' said the Tisroc in his deep, quiet voice. 'Every morning the sun is darkened in my eyes, and every night my sleep is the less refreshing, because I remember that Narnia is still free.'

'O my father,' said Rabadash. 'How if I show you a way by which you can stretch out your arm to take Narnia and yet draw it back unharmed if the attempt prove unfortunate?'

'If you can show me that, O Rabadash,' said the Tisroc, 'you will be the best of sons.'

'Hear then, O father. This very night and in this hour I will take but two hundred horse and ride across the desert. And it shall seem to all men that you know nothing of my going. On the second morning I shall be at the gates of King Lune's castle of Anvard in Archenland. They are at peace with us and unprepared and I shall take Anvard before they have bestirred themselves. Then I will ride through the pass above Anvard and down through Narnia to Cair Paravel. The High King will not be there; when I left them he was already preparing a raid against the giants on his northern border. I shall find Cair Paravel, most likely, with open gates and ride in. I shall exercise prudence and courtesy and spill as little Narnian blood as I can. And what then remains but to sit there till the *Splendour Hyaline* puts in, with Queen Susan on board, catch my strayed bird as she sets foot ashore, swing her into the saddle, and then ride, ride, ride back to Anvard?'

'But is it not probable, O my son,' said the Tisroc, 'that at the taking of the woman either King Edmund or you will lose his life?'

'They will be a small company,' said Rabadash, 'and I will order ten of my men to disarm and bind him: restraining my vehement desire for his blood so that there shall be no deadly cause of war between you and the High King.'

'And how if the *Splendour Hyaline* is at Cair Paravel before you?'

'I do not look for that with these winds, O my father.'

'And lastly, O my resourceful son,' said the Tisroc, 'you have made clear how all this might give you the barbarian woman, but not how it helps me to the overthrowing of Narnia.'

'O my father, can it have escaped you that though I and my horsemen will come and go through Narnia like an arrow from a bow, yet we shall have Anvard for ever? And when you hold Anvard you sit in the very gate of Narnia, and your garrison in Anvard can be increased by little and little till it is a great host.'

'It is spoken with understanding and foresight. But how do I draw back my arm if all this miscarries?'

'You shall say that I did it without your knowledge and against your will, and without your blessing, being constrained by the violence of my love and the impetuosity of youth.'

'And how if the High King then demands that we send back the barbarian woman, his sister?'

'O my father, be assured that he will not. For though the fancy of a woman has rejected this marriage, the High King Peter is a man of prudence and understanding who will in no way wish to lose the high honour and advantage of being allied to our House and seeing his nephew and grand nephew on the throne of Calormen.'

'He will not see that if I live for ever as is no doubt your wish,' said the Tisroc in an even drier voice than usual.

'And also, O my father and O the delight of my eyes,' said the Prince, after a moment of awkward silence, 'we shall write letters as if from the Queen to say that she loves me and has no desire to return to Narnia. For it is well known that women are as changeable as weather-cocks. And even if they do not wholly believe the letters, they will not dare to come to Tashbaan in arms to fetch her.'

'O enlightened Vizier,' said the Tisroc, 'bestow your wisdom upon us concerning this strange proposal.'

'O eternal Tisroc,' answered Ahoshta, 'the strength of paternal affection is not unknown to me and I have often heard that sons are in the eyes of their fathers more precious than carbuncles. How then shall I dare freely to unfold to you my mind in a matter which may imperil the life of this exalted Prince?'

'Undoubtedly you will dare,' replied the Tisroc. 'Because you will find that the dangers of not doing so are at least equally great.'

'To hear is to obey,' moaned the wretched man. 'Know then, O most reasonable Tisroc, in the first place, that the danger of the Prince is not altogether so great as might appear. For the gods have withheld from the barbarians the light of discretion, as that their poetry is not, like ours, full of choice apophthegms and useful maxims, but is all of love and war. Therefore nothing will appear to them more noble and admirable than such a mad enterprise as this of – ow!' For the Prince, at the word 'mad', had kicked him again.

'Desist, O my son,' said the Tisroc. 'And you, estimable

Vizier, whether he desists or not, by no means allow the flow of your eloquence to be interrupted. For nothing is more suitable to persons of gravity and decorum than to endure minor inconveniences with constancy.'

'To hear is to obey,' said the Vizier, wriggling himself round a little so as to get his hinder parts further away from Rabadash's toe. 'Nothing, I say, will seem as pardonable, if not estimable, in their eyes as this – er – hazardous attempt, especially because it is undertaken for the love of a woman. Therefore, if the Prince by misfortune fell into their hands, they would assuredly not kill him. Nay, it may even be, that though he failed to carry off the queen, yet the sight of his great valour and of the extremity of his passion might incline her heart to him.'

'That is a good point, old babbler,' said Rabadash. 'Very good, however it came into your ugly head.'

'The praise of my masters is the light of my eyes,' said Ahoshta. 'And secondly, O Tisroc, whose reign must and shall be interminable, I think that with the aid of the gods it is very likely that Anvard will fall into the Prince's hands. And if so, we have Narnia by the throat.'

There was a long pause and the room became so silent that the two girls hardly dared to breathe. At last the Tisroc spoke.

'Go, my son,' he said. 'And do as you have said. But expect no help nor countenance from me. I will not avenge you if you are killed and I will not deliver you if the barbarians cast you into prison. And if, either in success or failure, you shed a drop more than you need of Narnian noble blood and open war arises from it, my favour shall never fall upon you again and your next brother shall have your place in Calormen. Now go. Be swift, secret, and fortunate. May the strength of Tash the inexorable, the irresistible be in your sword and lance.'

'To hear is to obey,' cried Rabadash, and after kneeling for a moment to kiss his father's hands he rushed from the room. Greatly to the disappointment of Aravis, who was now horribly cramped, the Tisroc and the Vizier remained.

'O Vizier,' said the Tisroc, 'is it certain that no living soul knows of this council we three have held here tonight?'

'O my master,' said Ahoshta, 'it is not possible that any should know. For that very reason I proposed, and you in your wisdom agreed, that we should meet here in the Old Palace where no council is ever held and none of the household has any occasion to come.'

'It is well,' said the Tisroc. 'If any man knew, I would see to it that he died before an hour had passed. And do you also, O prudent Vizier, forget it. I sponge away from my own heart and from yours all knowledge of the Prince's plans. He is gone without my knowledge or my consent, I know not whither, because of his violence and the rash and disobedient disposition of youth. No man will be more astonished than you and I to hear that Anvard is in his hands.'

'To hear is to obey,' said Ahoshta.

'That is why you will never think even in your secret heart that I am the hardest hearted of fathers who thus send my first-born son on an errand so likely to be his death; pleasing as it must be to you who do not love the Prince. For I see into the bottom of your mind.'

'O impeccable Tisroc,' said the Vizier. 'In comparison with you I love neither the Prince nor my own life nor bread nor water nor the light of the sun.'

'Your sentiments,' said the Tisroc, 'are elevated and correct. I also love none of these things in comparison with the glory and strength of my throne. If the Prince succeeds, we have Archenland, and perhaps hereafter Narnia. If he fails – I have eighteen other sons and Raba- dash, after the manner of the eldest sons of kings, was beginning to be dangerous. More than five Tisrocs in Tashbaan have died before their time because their eldest sons, enlightened princes, grew tired of waiting for their throne. He had better cool his blood abroad than boil it in inaction here. And now, O excellent Vizier, the excess of my paternal anxiety inclines me to sleep. Command the musicians to my chamber. But before you lie down, call back the pardon we wrote for the third cook. I feel within me the manifest prognostics of indigestion.'

'To hear is to obey,' said the Grand Vizier. He crawled backwards on all fours to the door, rose, bowed, and went out. Even then the Tisroc remained seated in silence on the divan till Aravis almost began to be afraid that he had dropped asleep. But at last with a great creaking and sighing he heaved up his enormous body, signed to the slaves to precede him with the lights, and went out. The door closed behind him, the room was once more totally dark, and the two girls could breathe freely again.

CHAPTER 9

ACROSS THE DESERT

'How dreadful! How perfectly dreadful!' whimpered Lasaraleen. 'Oh darling, I *am* so frightened. I'm shaking all over. Feel me.'

'Come on,' said Aravis, who was trembling herself. 'They've gone back to the new palace. Once we're out of this room we're safe enough. But it's wasted a terrible time. Get me down to that water-gate as quick as you can'.

'Darling, how *can* you?' squeaked Lasaraleen. 'I can't do anything – not now. My poor nerves! No: we must just lie still a bit and then go back.'

'Why back?' asked Aravis.

'Oh, you don't understand. You're so unsympathetic,' said Lasaraleen, beginning to cry. Aravis decided it was no occasion for mercy.

'Look here!' she said, catching Lasaraleen and giving her a good shake. 'If you say another word about going back, and if you don't start taking me to that water-gate at once – do you know what I'll do? I'll rush out into that passage and scream. Then we'll both be caught.'

'But we shall both be k-k-killed!' said Lasaraleen. 'Didn't you hear what the Tisroc (may he live for ever) said?'

'Yes, and I'd sooner be killed than married to Ahoshta. So come *on*.'

'Oh you *are* unkind,' said Lasaraleen. 'And I in such a state!'

But in the end she had to give in to Aravis. She led the way down the steps they had already descended, and along another corridor and so finally out into the open air. They were now in the palace garden which sloped down in terraces to the city wall. The moon shone brightly. One of the drawbacks about adventures is that when you come to the most beautiful places you are often too anxious and hurried to appreciate them; so that Aravis (though she remembered them years later) had only a vague impression of grey lawns, quietly bubbling fountains, and the long black shadows of cypress trees.

When they reached the very bottom and the wall rose frowning above them, Lasaraleen was shaking so that she could not unbolt the gate. Aravis did it. There, at last, was the river, full of reflected moonlight, and a little landing stage and a few pleasure boats.

'Good-bye,' said Aravis, 'and thank you. I'm sorry if I've been a pig. But think what I'm flying from!'

'Oh Aravis darling,' said Lasaraleen. 'Won't you change your mind? Now that you've seen what a very great man Ahoshta is!'

'Great man!' said Aravis. 'A hideous grovelling slave who flatters when he's kicked but treasures it all up and hopes to get his own back by egging on that horrible Tisroc to plot his son's death. Faugh! I'd sooner marry my father's scullion than a creature like that.'

'Oh Aravis, Aravis! How can you say such dreadful things; and about the Tisroc (may he live for ever) too. It must be right if *he's* going to do it!'

'Good-bye,' said Aravis, 'and I thought your dresses lovely. And I think your house is lovely too. I'm sure you'll have a lovely life – though it wouldn't suit me. Close the door softly behind me.'

She tore herself away from her friend's affectionate embraces, stepped into a punt, cast off, and a moment later was out in midstream with a huge real moon overhead and a huge reflected moon down, deep down, in the river. The air was fresh and cool and as she drew near the farther bank she heard the hooting of an owl. 'Ah! That's better!' thought Aravis. She had always lived in the country and had hated every minute of her time in Tashbaan.

When she stepped ashore she found herself in darkness for the rise of the ground, and the trees, cut off the moonlight. But she managed to find the same road that Shasta had found, and came just as he had done to the end of the grass and the beginning of the sand, and looked (like him) to her left and saw the big, black Tombs. And now at last, brave girl though she was, her heart quailed. Supposing the others weren't there! Supposing the ghouls were! But she stuck out her chin (and a little bit of her tongue too) and went straight towards them.

But before she had reached them she saw Bree and Hwin and the groom.

'You can go back to your mistress now,' said Aravis (quite forgetting that he couldn't, until the city gates opened next morning). 'Here is money for your pains.'

'To hear is to obey,' said the groom, and at once set off at a remarkable speed in the direction of the city. There was no need to tell him to make haste: he also had been thinking a good deal about ghouls.

For the next few seconds Aravis was busy kissing the noses and patting the necks of Hwin and Bree just as if they were quite ordinary horses.

'And here comes Shasta! Thanks be to the Lion!' said Bree.

Aravis looked round, and there, right enough, was Shasta who had come out of hiding the moment he saw the groom going away.

'And now,' said Aravis. 'There's not a moment to lose.' And in hasty words she told them about Rabadash's expedition.

'Treacherous hounds!' said Bree, shaking his mane and stamping with his hoof. 'An attack in time of peace, without defiance sent! But we'll grease his oats for him. We'll be there before he is.'

'Can we?' said Aravis, swinging herself into Hwin's saddle. Shasta wished he could mount like that.

'Brooh-hoo!' snorted Bree. 'Up you get, Shasta. Can we! And with a good start too!'

'He said he was going to start at once,' said Aravis.

'That's how humans talk,' said Bree. 'But you don't get a company of two hundred horse and horsemen watered and victualled and armed and saddled and started all in a minute. Now: what's our direction? Due North?'

'No,' said Shasta. 'I know about that. I've drawn a line. I'll explain later. Bear a bit to our left, both you horses. Ah – here it is!'

'Now,' said Bree. 'All that about galloping for a day and a night, like in stories, can't really be done. It must be walk and trot: but brisk trots and short walks. And whenever we walk you two humans can slip off and walk too. Now. Are you ready, Hwin? Off we go. Narnia and the North!'

At first it was delightful. The night had now been going on for so many hours that the sand had almost finished giving back all the sun-heat it had received during the day, and the air was cool, fresh, and clear. Under the moonlight the sand, in every direction and as far as they could see, gleamed as if it were smooth water or a great silver tray. Except for the noise of Bree's and Hwin's hoofs there was not a sound to be heard. Shasta would nearly have fallen asleep if he had not had to dismount and walk every now and then.

This seemed to last for hours. Then there came a time when there was no longer any moon. They seemed to ride in the dead darkness for hours and hours. And after that there came a moment when Shasta noticed that he could see Bree's neck and head in front of him a little more clearly than before; and slowly, very slowly, he began to notice the vast grey flatness on every side. It looked absolutely dead, like something in a dead world; and Shasta felt quite terribly tired and noticed that he was getting cold and that his lips were dry. And all the time the squeak of the leather, the jingle of the bits, and the noise of the hoofs – not *Propputty-propputty* as it would be on a hard road, but *Thubbudy-thubbudy* on the dry sand.

At last, after hours of riding, far away on his right there came a single long streak of paler grey, low down on the horizon. Then a streak of red. It was the morning at last, but without a single bird to sing about it. He was glad of the walking bits now, for he was colder than ever.

Then suddenly the sun rose and everything changed in a moment. The grey sand turned yellow and twinkled as if it was strewn with diamonds. On their left the shadows of Shasta and Hwin and Bree and Aravis, enormously long, raced beside them. The double peak of Mount Pire, far ahead, flashed in the sunlight and Shasta saw they were a

little out of the course. 'A bit left, a bit left,' he sang out.
Best of all, when you looked back, Tashbaan was already
small and remote. The Tombs were quite invisible: swal-
lowed up in that single, jagged-edged hump which was the
city of the Tisroc. Everyone felt better.

But not for long. Though Tashbaan looked very far
away when they first saw it, it refused to look any further
away as they went on. Shasta gave up looking back at it,
for it only gave him the feeling that they were not moving
at all. Then the light became a nuisance. The glare of the
sand made his eyes ache: but he knew he mustn't shut them.
He must screw them up and keep on looking ahead at
Mount Pire and shouting out directions. Then came the
heat. He noticed it for the first time when he had to dismount and walk: as he slipped down to the sand the heat
from it struck up into his face as if from the opening of an
oven door. Next time it was worse. But the third time, as
his bare feet touched the sand he screamed with pain and
got one foot back in the stirrup and the other half over
Bree's back before you could have said knife.

'Sorry, Bree,' he gasped. 'I can't walk. It burns my feet.'

'Of course!' panted Bree. 'Should have thought of
that myself. Stay on. Can't be helped.'

'It's all right for *you*,' said Shasta to Aravis who was
walking beside Hwin. 'You've got shoes on.'

Aravis said nothing and looked prim. Let's hope she
didn't mean to, but she did.

On again, trot and walk and trot, jingle-jingle-jingle,
squeak-squeak-squeak, smell of hot horse, smell of hot self,
blinding glare, headache. And nothing at all different for
mile after mile. Tashbaan would never look any further
away. The mountains would never look any nearer. You

felt this had been going on for always – jingle-jingle-jingle, squeak-squeak-squeak, smell of hot horse, smell of hot self.

Of course one tried all sorts of games with oneself to try to make the time pass: and of course they were all no good. And one tried very hard not to think of drinks – iced sherbet in a palace at Tashbaan, clear spring water tinkling with a dark earthy sound, cold, smooth milk just creamy enough and not too creamy – and the harder you tried not to think, the more you thought.

At last there was something different – a mass of rock sticking up out of the sand about fifty yards long and thirty feet high. It did not cast much shadow, for the sun was now very high, but it cast a little. Into that shade they crowded. There they ate some food and drank a little water. It is not easy giving a horse a drink out of a skin bottle, but Bree and Hwin were clever with their lips. No one had anything like enough. No one spoke. The Horses were flecked with foam and their breathing was noisy. The children were pale.

After a very short rest they went on again. Same noises, same smells, same glare, till at last their shadows began to fall on their right, and then got longer and longer till they seemed to stretch out to the eastern end of the world. Very slowly the sun drew nearer to the Western horizon. And now at last he was down and, thank goodness, the merciless glare was gone, though the heat coming up from the sand was still as bad as ever. Four pairs of eyes were looking out eagerly for any sign of the valley that Sallowpad the Raven had spoken about. But, mile after mile, there was nothing but level sand. And now the day was quite definitely done, and most of the stars were out, and still the

Horses thundered on and the children rose and sank in their saddles, miserable with thirst and weariness. Not till

the moon had risen did Shasta – in the strange, barking voice of someone whose mouth is perfectly dry – shout out:

'There it is!'

There was no mistaking it now. Ahead, and a little to their right, there was at last a slope: a slope downward and hummocks of rock on each side. The Horses were far too tired to speak but they swung round towards it and in a minute or two they were entering the gully. At first it was worse in there than it had been out in the open desert, for there was a breathless stuffiness between the rocky walls and less moonlight. The slope continued steeply downwards and the rocks on either hand rose to the height of cliffs. Then they began to meet vegetation – prickly cactus-like plants and coarse grass of the kind that would prick your fingers. Soon the horse-hoofs were falling on pebbles and stones instead of sand. Round every bend of the valley – and it had many bends – they looked eagerly for water. The Horses were nearly at the end of their strength now, and Hwin, stumbling and panting, was

lagging behind Bree. They were almost in despair before at last they came to a little muddiness and a tiny trickle of water through softer and better grass. And the trickle became a brook, and the brook became a stream with bushes on each side, and the stream became a river, and there came (after more disappointments than I could possibly describe) a moment when Shasta, who had been in a kind of doze, suddenly realized that Bree had stopped and found himself slipping off. Before them a little cataract of water poured into a broad pool: and both the Horses were already in the pool with their heads down, drinking, drinking, drinking. 'O-o-oh,' said Shasta and plunged in – it was about up to his knees – and stooped his head right into the cataract. It was perhaps the loveliest moment in his life.

It was about ten minutes later when all four of them (the two children wet nearly all over) came out and began to notice their surroundings. The moon was now high enough to peep down into the valley. There was soft grass on both sides of the river, and beyond the grass, trees and bushes sloped up to the bases of the cliffs. There must have been some wonderful flowering shrubs hidden in that shadowy undergrowth for the whole glade was full of the coolest and most delicious smells. And out of the darkest recess among the trees there came a sound Shasta had never heard before – a nightingale.

Everyone was much too tired to speak or to eat. The Horses, without waiting to be unsaddled, lay down at once. So did Aravis and Shasta.

About ten minutes later the careful Hwin said, 'But we mustn't go to sleep. We've got to keep ahead of that Rabadash.'

'No,' said Bree very slowly. 'Mustn't go sleep. Just a little rest.'

Shasta knew (for a moment) that they would all go to sleep if he didn't get up and do something about it, and felt that he ought to. In fact he decided that he would get up and persuade them to go on. But presently; not yet: not just yet. . . .

Very soon the moon shone and the nightingale sang over two horses and two human children, all fast asleep.

It was Aravis who awoke first. The sun was already high

in the heavens and the cool morning hours were already wasted. 'It's my fault,' she said to herself furiously as she jumped up and began rousing the others. 'One wouldn't expect Horses to keep awake after a day's work like that, even if they *can* talk. And of course that Boy wouldn't; he's had no decent training. But *I* ought to have known better.'

The others were dazed and stupid with the heaviness of their sleep.

'Heigh-ho – broo-hoo,' said Bree. 'Been sleeping in my saddle, eh? I'll never do that again. Most uncomfortable –'

'Oh come on, come on,' said Aravis. 'We've lost half the morning already. There isn't a moment to spare.'

'A fellow's got to have a mouthful of grass,' said Bree.

'I'm afraid we can't wait,' said Aravis.

'What's the terrible hurry?' said Bree. 'We've crossed the desert, haven't we?'

'But we're not in Archenland yet,' said Aravis. 'And we've got to get there before Rabadash.'

'Oh, we must be miles ahead of him,' said Bree. 'Haven't we been coming a shorter way? Didn't that Raven friend of yours say this was a short cut, Shasta?'

'He didn't say anything about *shorter*,' answered Shasta. 'He only said *better*, because you got to a river this way. If the oasis is due North of Tashbaan, then I'm afraid this may be longer.'

'Well I can't go on without a snack,' said Bree. 'Take my bridle off, Shasta.'

'P-please,' said Hwin, very shyly, 'I feel just like Bree that I *can't* go on. But when Horses have humans (with spurs and things) on their backs, aren't they often made to go on when they're feeling like this? and then they find they can. I m-mean – oughtn't we to be able to do even more, now that we're free. It's all for Narnia.'

'I think, Ma'am,' said Bree very crushingly, 'that I know a little more about campaigns and forced marches and what a horse can stand than you do.'

To this Hwin made no answer, being, like most highly bred mares, a very nervous and gentle person who was easily put down. In reality she was quite right, and if Bree had had a Tarkaan on his back at that moment to make him go on, he would have found that he was good for several hours' hard going. But one of the worst results of being a slave and being forced to do things is that when there is no one to force you any more you find you have almost lost the power of forcing yourself.

So they had to wait while Bree had a snack and a drink, and of course Hwin and the children had a snack and a drink too. It must have been nearly eleven o'clock in the morning before they finally got going again. And even then Bree took things much more gently than yesterday. It was really Hwin, though she was the weaker and more tired of the two, who set the pace.

The valley itself, with its brown, cool river, and grass and moss and wild flowers and rhododendrons, was such a pleasant place that it made you want to ride slowly.

CHAPTER 10

THE HERMIT OF THE
SOUTHERN MARCH

AFTER they had ridden for several hours down the valley, it widened out and they could see what was ahead of them. The river which they had been following here joined a broader river, wide and turbulent, which flowed from their left to their right, towards the east. Beyond this new river a delightful country rose gently in low hills, ridge beyond ridge, to the Northern Mountains themselves. To the right there were rocky pinnacles, one or two of them with snow clinging to the ledges. To the left, pine-clad slopes, frowning cliffs, narrow gorges, and blue peaks stretched away as far as the eye could reach. He could no longer make out Mount Pire. Straight ahead the mountain range sank to a wooded saddle which of course must be the pass from Archenland into Narnia.

'Broo-hoo-hoo, the North, the green North!' neighed Bree: and certainly the lower hills looked greener and fresher than anything that Aravis and Shasta, with their southern-bred eyes, had ever imagined. Spirits rose as they clattered down to the water's-meet of the two rivers.

The eastern-flowing river, which was pouring from the higher mountains at the western end of the range, was far too swift and too broken with rapids for them to think of swimming it; but after some casting about, up and down the bank, they found a place shallow enough to wade. The roar and clatter of water, the great swirl against the horses' fetlocks, the cool, stirring air and the darting dragon-flies, filled Shasta with a strange excitement.

'Friends, we are in Archenland!' said Bree proudly as he splashed and churned his way out on the Northern bank. 'I think that river we've just crossed is called the Winding Arrow.'

'I hope we're in time,' murmured Hwin.

Then they began going up, slowly and zigzagging a good deal, for the hills were steep. It was all open park-like country with no roads or houses in sight. Scattered trees, never thick enough to be a forest, were everywhere. Shasta, who had lived all his life in an almost tree-less grassland, had never seen so many or so many kinds. If you had been there you would probably have known (he didn't) that he was seeing oaks, beeches, silver birches, rowans, and sweet chestnuts. Rabbits scurried away in every direction as they advanced, and presently they saw a whole herd of fallow deer making off among the trees.

'Isn't it simply glorious!' said Aravis.

At the first ridge Shasta turned in the saddle and looked back. There was no sign of Tashbaan; the desert, unbroken except by the narrow green crack which they had travelled down, spread to the horizon.

'Hullo!' he said suddenly. 'What's that!'

'What's what?' said Bree, turning round. Hwin and Aravis did the same.

'That,' said Shasta, pointing. 'It looks like smoke. Is it a fire?'

'Sand-storm, I should say,' said Bree.

'Not much wind to raise it,' said Aravis.

'Oh!' exclaimed Hwin. 'Look! There are things flashing

in it. Look! They're helmets – and armour. And it's moving: moving this way.'

'By Tash!' said Aravis. 'It's the army. It's Rabadash.'

'Oh course it is,' said Hwin. 'Just what I was afraid of. Quick! We must get to Anvard before it.' And without another word she whisked round and began galloping North. Bree tossed his head and did the same.

'Come *on*, Bree, come on,' yelled Aravis over her shoulder.

This race was very gruelling for the Horses. As they topped each ridge they found another valley and another ridge beyond it; and though they knew they were going in more or less the right direction, no one knew how far it was to Anvard. From the top of the second ridge Shasta looked back again. Instead of a dust-cloud well out in the desert he now saw a black, moving mass, rather like ants, on the far bank of the Winding Arrow. They were doubtless looking for a ford.

'They're on the river!' he yelled wildly.

'Quick! Quick!' shouted Aravis. 'We might as well not have come at all if we don't reach Anvard in time. Gallop, Bree, gallop. Remember you're a war-horse.'

It was all Shasta could do to prevent himself from shouting out similar instructions; but he thought, 'The poor chap's doing all he can already,' and held his tongue. And certainly both Horses were doing, if not all they could, all they thought they could; which is not quite the same thing. Bree had caught up with Hwin and they thundered side by side over the turf. It didn't look as if Hwin could possibly keep it up much longer.

At that moment everyone's feelings were completely altered by a sound from behind. It was not the sound they had been expecting to hear – the noise of hoofs and jingling armour, mixed, perhaps, with Calormene battle-cries. Yet Shasta knew it at once. It was the same snarling roar he had heard that moonlit night when they first met Aravis and Hwin. Bree knew it too. His eyes gleamed red and his ears lay flat back on his skull. And Bree now discovered that he had not really been going as fast – not quite as fast – as he could. Shasta felt the change at once. Now they were really going all out. In a few seconds they were well ahead of Hwin.

'It's not fair,' thought Shasta. 'I *did* think we'd be safe from lions here!'

He looked over his shoulder. Everything was only too clear. A huge tawny creature, its body low to the ground, like a cat streaking across the lawn to a tree when a strange dog has got into the garden, was behind them. And it was nearer every second and half second.

He looked forward again and saw something which he did not take in, or even think about. Their way was barred by a smooth green wall about ten feet high. In the middle of that wall there was a gate, open. In the middle of the gateway stood a tall man dressed, down to his bare feet, in a robe coloured like autumn leaves, leaning on a straight staff. His beard fell almost to his knees.

Shasta saw all this in a glance and looked back again. The lion had almost got Hwin now. It was making snaps at her hind legs, and there was no hope now in her foam-flecked, wide-eyed face.

'Stop,' bellowed Shasta in Bree's ear. 'Must go back. Must help!'

Bree always said afterwards that he never heard, or never understood this; and as he was in general a very truthful horse we must accept his word.

Shasta slipped his feet out of the stirrups, slid both his legs over on the left side, hesitated for one hideous hundredth of a second, and jumped. It hurt horribly and nearly winded him; but before he knew how it hurt him he was staggering back to help Aravis. He had never done anything like this in his life before and hardly knew why he was doing it now.

One of the most terrible noises in the world, a horse's scream, broke from Hwin's lips. Aravis was stooping low over Hwin's neck and seemed to be trying to draw her sword. And now all three – Aravis, Hwin, and the lion –

were almost on top of Shasta. Before they reached him the lion rose on its hind legs, larger than you would have believed a lion could be, and jabbed at Aravis with its right paw. Shasta could see all the terrible claws extended. Aravis screamed and reeled in the saddle. The lion was tearing her shoulders. Shasta, half mad with horror, managed to lurch towards the brute. He had no weapon, not even a stick or a stone. He shouted out, idiotically, at the lion as one would at a dog. 'Go home! Go home!' For a fraction of a second he was staring right into its wide-opened, raging mouth. Then, to his utter astonishment, the lion, still on its hind legs, checked itself suddenly, turned head over heels, picked itself up, and rushed away.

Shasta did not for a moment suppose it had gone for good. He turned and raced for the gate in the green wall which, now for the first time, he remembered seeing. Hwin, stumbling and nearly fainting, was just entering the gate: Aravis still kept her seat but her back was covered with blood.

'Come in, my daughter, come in,' the robed and bearded man was saying, and then 'Come in, my son' as Shasta panted up to him. He heard the gate closed behind him; and the bearded stranger was already helping Aravis off her horse.

They were in a wide and perfectly circular enclosure, protected by a high wall of green turf. A pool of perfectly still water, so full that the water was almost exactly level with the ground, lay before him. At one end of the pool, completely overshadowing it with its branches, there grew the hugest and most beautiful tree that Shasta had ever seen. Beyond the pool was a little low house of stone roofed

with deep and ancient thatch. There was a sound of bleat-
ing and over at the far side of the enclosure there were some
goats. The level ground was completely covered with the
finest grass.

'Are – are – are you,' panted Shasta. 'Are you King Lune
of Archenland?'

The old man shook his head. 'No,' he replied in a quiet
voice, 'I am the Hermit of the Southern March. And now,
my son, waste no time on questions, but obey. This damsel
is wounded. Your horses are spent. Rabadash is at this
moment finding a ford over the Winding Arrow. If you
run now, without a moment's rest, you will still be in time
to warn King Lune.'

Shasta's heart fainted at these words for he felt he had
no strength left. And he writhed inside at what seemed
the cruelty and unfairness of the demand. He had not yet
learned that if you do one good deed your reward usually
is to be set to do another and harder and better one. But all
he said out loud was:

'Where is the King?'

The Hermit turned and pointed with his staff. 'Look,'
he said. 'There is another gate, right opposite to the
one you entered by. Open it and go straight ahead:
always straight ahead, over level or steep, over smooth
or rough, over dry or wet. I know by my art that you
will find King Lune straight ahead. But run, run:
always run.'

Shasta nodded his head, ran to the northern gate and disappeared beyond it. Then the Hermit took Aravis, whom
he had all this time been supporting with his left arm, and
half led, half carried her into the house. After a long time
he came out again.

'Now, cousins,' he said to the Horses. 'It is your turn.'

Without waiting for an answer – and indeed they were too exhausted to speak – he took the bridles and saddles off both of them. Then he rubbed them both down, so well that a groom in a King's stable could not have done it better.

'There, cousins,' he said, 'dismiss it all from your minds and be comforted. Here is water and there is grass. You shall have a hot mash when I have milked my other cousins, the goats.'

'Sir,' said Hwin, finding her voice at last, 'will the Tarkheena live? Has the lion killed her?'

'I who know many present things by my art,' replied the Hermit with a smile, 'have yet little knowledge of things future. Therefore I do not know whether any man or woman or beast in the whole world will be alive when the sun sets tonight. But be of good hope. The damsel is likely to live as long as any of her age.'

When Aravis came to herself she found that she was lying on her face on a low bed of extraordinary softness in a cool, bare room with walls of undressed stone. She couldn't understand why she had been laid on her face; but when she tried to turn and felt the hot, burning pains all over her back, she remembered, and realized why. She couldn't understand what delightfully springy stuff the bed was made of, because it was made of heather (which is the best bedding) and heather was a thing she had never seen or heard of.

The door opened and the Hermit entered, carrying a large wooden bowl in his hand. After carefully setting this down, he came to the bedside, and asked:

'How do you find yourself, my daughter?'

'My back is very sore, father,' said Aravis, 'but there is nothing else wrong with me.'

He knelt beside her, laid his hand on her forehead, and felt her pulse.

'There is no fever,' he said. 'You will do well. Indeed there is no reason why you should not get up tomorrow. But now, drink this.'

He fetched the wooden bowl and held it to her lips. Aravis couldn't help making a face when she tasted it, for goats' milk is rather a shock when you are not used to it. But she was very thirsty and managed to drink it all and felt better when she had finished.

'Now, daughter, you may sleep when you wish,' said the Hermit. 'For your wounds are washed and dressed and though they smart they are no more serious than if they had been the cuts of a whip. It must have been a very strange lion; for instead of catching you out of the saddle and getting his teeth into you, he has only drawn his claws across your back. Ten scratches: sore, but not deep or dangerous.'

'I say!' said Aravis. 'I *have* had luck.'

'Daughter,' said the Hermit, 'I have now lived a hundred and nine winters in this world and have never yet met any such thing as Luck. There is something about all this that I do not understand: but if ever we need to know it, you may be sure that we shall.'

'And what about Rabadash and his two hundred horse?' asked Aravis.

'They will not pass this way, I think,' said the Hermit. 'They must have found a ford by now well to the east of us. From there they will try to ride straight to Anvard.'

'Poor Shasta!' said Aravis. 'Has he far to go? Will he get there first?'

'There is good hope of it,' said the old man.

Aravis lay down again (on her side this time) and said, 'Have I been asleep for a long time? It seems to be getting dark.'

The Hermit was looking out of the only window, which faced north. 'This is not the darkness of night,' he said presently. 'The clouds are rolling down from Stormness Head. Our foul weather always comes from there in these parts. There will be thick fog tonight.'

Next day, except for her sore back, Aravis felt so well that after breakfast (which was porridge and cream) the Hermit said she could get up. And of course she at once went out to speak to the Horses. The weather had changed and the whole of that green enclosure was filled, like a great green cup, with sunlight. It was a very peaceful place, lonely and quiet.

Hwin at once trotted across to Aravis and gave her a horse-kiss.

'But where's Bree?' said Aravis when each had asked after the other's health and sleep.

'Over there,' said Hwin, pointing with her nose to the far side of the circle. 'And I wish you'd come and talk to him. There's something wrong, I can't get a word out of him.'

They strolled across and found Bree lying with his face towards the wall, and though he must have heard them coming, he never turned his head or spoke a word.

'Good morning, Bree,' said Aravis. 'How are you this morning?'

Bree muttered something that no one could hear.

'The Hermit says that Shasta probably got to King Lune in time,' continued Aravis, 'so it looks as if all our troubles were over. Narnia, at last, Bree!'

'I shall never see Narnia,' said Bree in a low voice.

'Aren't you well, Bree dear?' said Aravis.

Bree turned round at last, his face mournful as only a horse's can be.

'I shall go back to Calormen,' he said.

'What?' said Aravis. 'Back to slavery!'

'Yes,' said Bree. 'Slavery is all I'm fit for. How can I ever show my face among the free Horses of Narnia? – I who left a mare and a girl and a boy to be eaten by lions while I galloped all I could to save my own wretched skin!'

'We all ran as hard as we could,' said Hwin.

'Shasta didn't!' snorted Bree. 'At least he ran in the right direction: ran *back*. And that is what shames me most of all. I, who called myself a war-horse and boasted of a hundred fights, to be beaten by a little human boy – a child, a mere foal, who had never held a sword nor had any good nurture or example in his life!'

'I know,' said Aravis. 'I felt just the same. Shasta was marvellous. I'm just as bad as you, Bree. I've been snubbing him and looking down on him ever since you met us and now he turns out to be the best of us all. But I think it would be better to stay and say we're sorry than to go back to Calormen.'

'It's all very well for you,' said Bree. 'You haven't disgraced yourself. But I've lost everything.'

'My good Horse,' said the Hermit, who had approached them unnoticed because his bare feet made so little noise on that sweet, dewy grass. 'My good Horse, you've lost nothing but your self-conceit. No, no, cousin. Don't put back your ears and shake your mane at me. If you are really so humbled as you sounded a minute ago, you must learn to listen to sense. You're not quite the great Horse you had come to think, from living among poor dumb horses. Of course you were braver and cleverer than *them*. You could hardly help being that. It doesn't follow that you'll be anyone very special in Narnia. But as long as you know you're nobody very special, you'll be a very decent sort of Horse, on the whole, and taking one thing with another. And now, if you and my other four-footed cousin will come round to the kitchen door we'll see about the other half of that mash.'

CHAPTER 11

THE UNWELCOME FELLOW TRAVELLER

WHEN Shasta went through the gate he found a slope of grass and a little heather running up before him to some trees. He had nothing to think about now and no plans to make: he had only to run, and that was quite enough. His limbs were shaking, a terrible stitch was beginning in his side, and the sweat that kept dropping into his eyes blinded them and made them smart. He was unsteady on his feet too, and more than once he nearly turned his ankle on a loose stone.

The trees were thicker now than they had yet been and in the more open spaces there was bracken. The sun had

gone in without making it any cooler. It had become one
of those hot, grey days when there seem to be twice as
many flies as usual. Shasta's face was covered with them; he
didn't even try to shake them off – he had too much else to
do.

Suddenly he heard a horn – not a great throbbing horn
like the horns of Tashbaan but a merry call, Ti-ro-to-to-ho!
Next moment he came out into a wide glade and found
himself in a crowd of people.

At least, it looked a crowd to him. In reality there were
about fifteen or twenty of them, all gentlemen in green
hunting-dress, with their horses; some in the saddle and
some standing by their horses' heads. In the centre someone was holding the stirrup for a man to mount. And the
man he was holding it for was the jolliest, fat, apple-
cheeked, twinkling-eyed King you could imagine.

As soon as Shasta came in sight this King forgot all about
mounting his horse. He spread out his arms to Shasta, his
face lit up, and he cried out in a great, deep voice that
seemed to come from the bottom of his chest:

'Corin! My son! And on foot, and in rags! What –'

'No,' panted Shasta, shaking his head. 'Not Prince
Corin. I – I – know I'm like him . . . saw his Highness in
Tashbaan . . . sent his greetings.'

The King was staring at Shasta with an extraordinary
expression on his face.

'Are you K-King Lune?' gasped Shasta. And then,
without waiting for an answer, 'Lord King – fly – Anvard
– shut the gates – enemies upon you – Rabadash and two
hundred horse.'

'Have you assurance of this, boy?' asked one of the
other gentlemen.

'My own eyes,' said Shasta. 'I've seen them. Raced them all the way from Tashbaan.'

'On foot?' said the gentleman, raising his eyebrows a little.

'Horses – with the Hermit,' said Shasta.

'Question him no more, Darrin,' said King Lune. 'I see

truth in his face. We must ride for it, gentlemen. A spare horse there, for the boy. You can ride fast, friend?'

For answer Shasta put his foot in the stirrup of the horse which had been led towards him and a moment later he was in the saddle. He had done it a hundred times with Bree in the last few weeks, and his mounting was very different now from what it had been on that first night when Bree had said that he climbed up a horse as if he were climbing a haystack.

He was pleased to hear the Lord Darrin say to the King, 'The boy has a true horseman's seat, Sire. I'll warrant there's noble blood in him.'

'His blood, aye, there's the point,' said the King. And he stared hard at Shasta again with that curious expression, almost a hungry expression, in his steady, grey eyes.

But by now the whole party was moving off at a brisk canter. Shasta's seat was excellent but he was sadly puzzled what to do with his reins, for he had never touched the reins while he was on Bree's back. But he looked very carefully out of the corners of his eyes to see what the others were doing (as some of us have done at parties when we weren't quite sure which knife or fork we were meant to use) and tried to get his fingers right. But he didn't dare to try really directing the horse; he trusted it would follow the rest. The horse was of course an ordinary horse, not a Talking Horse; but it had quite wits enough to realize that the strange boy on its back had no whip and no spurs and was not really master of the situation. That was why Shasta soon found himself at the tail end of the procession.

Even so, he was going pretty fast. There were no flies now and the air in his face was delicious. He had got his breath back too. And his errand had succeeded. For the first time since the arrival at Tashbaan (how long ago it seemed!) he was beginning to enjoy himself.

He looked up to see how much nearer the mountain tops had come. To his disappointment he could not see them at all: only a vague greyness, rolling down towards them. He had never been in mountain country before and was surprised. 'It's a cloud,' he said to himself, 'a cloud coming down. I see. Up here in the hills one is really in the sky. I shall see what the inside of a cloud is like. What fun!

I've often wondered.' Far away on his left, and a little behind him, the sun was getting ready to set.

They had come to a rough kind of road by now and were making very good speed. But Shasta's horse was still the last of the lot. Once or twice when the road made a bend (there was now continuous forest on each side of it) he lost sight of the others for a second or two.

Then they plunged into the fog, or else the fog rolled over them. The world became grey. Shasta had not realized how cold and wet the inside of a cloud would be; nor how dark. The grey turned to black with alarming speed.

Someone at the head of the column winded the horn every now and then, and each time the sound came from a little farther off. He couldn't see any of the others now, but of course he'd be able to as soon as he got round the next bend. But when he rounded it he still couldn't see them. In fact he could see nothing at all. His horse was walking now. 'Get on, Horse, get on,' said Shasta. Then came the horn, very faint. Bree had always told him that he must keep his heels well turned out, and Shasta had got the idea that something very terrible would happen if he dug his heels into a horse's sides. This seemed to him an occasion for trying it. 'Look here, Horse,' he said, 'if you don't buck up, do you know what I'll do? I'll dig my heels into you. I really will.' The horse, however, took no notice of this threat. So Shasta settled himself firmly in the saddle, gripped with his knees, clenched his teeth, and punched both the horse's sides with his heels as hard as he could.

The only result was that the horse broke into a kind of pretence of a trot for five or six paces and then subsided into a walk again. And now it was quite dark and they seemed to have given up blowing that horn. The only sound was a steady drip-drip from the branches of the trees.

'Well, I suppose even a walk will get us somewhere sometime,' said Shasta to himself. 'I only hope I shan't run into Rabadash and his people.'

He went on for what seemed a long time, always at a walking pace. He began to hate that horse, and he was also beginning to feel very hungry.

Presently he came to a place where the road divided into two. He was just wondering which led to Anvard when he was startled by a noise from behind him. It was the noise of trotting horses. 'Rabadash!' thought Shasta. He had no way of guessing which road Rabadash would take. 'But if I take one,' said Shasta to himself, 'he *may* take the other: and if I stay at the cross-roads I'm *sure* to be caught.' He dismounted and led his horse as quickly as he could along the right-hand road.

The sound of the cavalry grew rapidly nearer and in a minute or two Shasta realized that they were at the cross-roads. He held his breath, waiting to see which way they would take.

There came a low word of command 'Halt!' then a moment of horsey noises – nostrils blowing, hoofs pawing, bits being champed, necks being patted. Then a voice spoke.

'Attend, all of you,' it said. 'We are now within a furlong of the castle. Remember your orders. Once we are in Narnia, as we should be by sunrise, you are to kill as little as possible. On this venture you are to regard every drop of Narnian blood as more precious than a gallon of your own. On *this* venture, I say. The gods will send us a happier hour and then you must leave nothing alive between Cair Paravel and the Western Waste. But we are not yet in

Narnia. Here in Archenland it is another thing. In the
assault on this castle of King Lune's, nothing matters but
speed. Show your mettle. It must be mine within an hour.
And if it is, I give it all to you. I reserve no booty for myself.
Kill me every barbarian male within its walls, down to the
child that was born yesterday, and everything else is yours
to divide as you please – the women, the gold, the jewels,
the weapons, and the wine. The man that I see hanging
back when we come to the gates shall be burned alive. In
the name of Tash the irresistible, the inexorable – forward!'

With a great cloppitty-clop the column began to move,
and Shasta breathed again. They had taken the other road.

Shasta thought they took a long time going past, for
though he had been talking and thinking about 'two
hundred horse' all day, he had not realized how many they
really were. But at last the sound died away and once more
he was alone amid the drip-drip from the trees.

He now knew the way to Anvard but of course he could
not now go there: that would only mean running into the
arms of Rabadash's troopers. 'What on earth am I to do?'
said Shasta to himself. But he remounted his horse and
continued along the road he had chosen , in the faint hope
of finding some cottage where he might ask for shelter and
a meal. He had thought, of course, of going back to Aravis
and Bree and Hwin at the hermitage, but he couldn't
because by now he had not the least idea of the direction.

'After all,' said Shasta, 'this road is bound to get to
somewhere.'

But that all depends on what you mean by somewhere.
The road kept on getting to somewhere in the sense that
it got to more and more trees, all dark and dripping, and
to colder and colder air. And strange, icy winds kept

blowing the mist past him though they never blew it away.
If he had been used to mountain country he would have
realized that this meant he was now very high up – perhaps
right at the top of the pass. But Shasta knew nothing about
mountains.

'I *do* think,' said Shasta, 'that I must be the most unfortunate boy that ever lived in the whole world. Everything
goes right for everyone except me. Those Narnian lords
and ladies got safe away from Tashbaan; I was left behind.
Aravis and Bree and Hwin are all as snug as anything with
that old Hermit: of course I was the one who was sent on.
King Lune and his people must have got safely into the
castle and shut the gates long before Rabadash arrived,
but I get left out.'

And being very tired and having nothing inside him, he
felt so sorry for himself that the tears rolled down his
cheeks.

What put a stop to all this was a sudden fright. Shasta
discovered that someone or somebody was walking beside
him. It was pitch dark and he could see nothing. And the
Thing (or Person) was going so quietly that he could
hardly hear any footfalls. What he could hear was breathing. His invisible companion seemed to breathe on a very
large scale, and Shasta got the impression that it was a very
large creature. And he had come to notice this breathing so
gradually that he had really no idea how long it had been
there. It was a horrible shock.

It darted into his mind that he had heard long ago that
there were giants in these Northern countries. He bit his
lip in terror. But now that he really had something to cry
about, he stopped crying.

The Thing (unless it was a Person) went on beside him

so very quietly that Shasta began to hope he had only imagined it. But just as he was becoming quite sure of it, there suddenly came a deep, rich sigh out of the darkness beside him. That couldn't be imagination! Anyway, he had felt the hot breath of that sigh on his chilly left hand.

If the horse had been any good – or if he had known how to get any good out of the horse – he would have risked everything on a break away and a wild gallop. But he knew he couldn't make that horse gallop. So he went on at a walking pace and the unseen companion walked and breathed beside him. At last he could bear it no longer.

'Who are you?' he said, scarcely above a whisper.

'One who has waited long for you to speak,' said the Thing. Its voice was not loud, but very large and deep.

'Are you – are you a giant?' asked Shasta.

'You might call me a giant,' said the Large Voice. 'But I am not like the creatures you call giants.'

'I can't see you at all,' said Shasta, after staring very hard. Then (for an even more terrible idea had come into his head) he said, almost in a scream, 'You're not – not something *dead*, are you? Oh please – please do go away. What harm have I ever done you? Oh, I am the unluckiest person in the whole world?'

Once more he felt the warm breath of the Thing on his hand and face. 'There,' it said, 'that is not the breath of a ghost. Tell me your sorrows.'

Shasta was a little reassured by the breath: so he told how he had never known his real father or mother and had been brought up sternly by the fisherman. And then he told the story of his escape and how they were chased by lions and forced to swim for their lives; and of all their dangers in Tashbaan and about his night among the Tombs and how the beasts howled at him out of the desert. And he told about the heat and thirst of their desert journey and how they were almost at their goal when another lion chased them and wounded Aravis. And also, how very long it was since he had had anything to eat.

'I do not call you unfortunate,' said the Large Voice.

'Don't you think it was bad luck to meet so many lions?' said Shasta.

'There was only one lion,' said the Voice.

'What on earth do you mean? I've just told you there were at least two the first night, and –'

'There was only one: but he was swift of foot.'

'How do you know?'

'I was the lion.' And as Shasta gaped with open mouth and said nothing, the Voice continued. 'I was the lion who forced you to join with Aravis. I was the cat who comforted you among the houses of the dead. I was the lion who drove the jackals from you while you slept. I was the lion who gave the Horses the new strength of fear for the last mile so that you should reach King Lune in time. And I was the lion you do not remember who pushed the boat in which you lay, a child near death, so that it came to shore where a man sat, wakeful at midnight, to receive you.'

'Then it was you who wounded Aravis?'

'It was I.'

'But what for?'

'Child,' said the Voice, 'I am telling you your story, not hers. I tell no one any story but his own.'

'Who *are* you?' asked Shasta.

'Myself,' said the Voice, very deep and low so that the earth shook: and again 'Myself,' loud and clear and gay: and then the third time 'Myself', whispered so softly you could hardly hear it, and yet it seemed to come from all round you as if the leaves rustled with it.

Shasta was no longer afraid that the Voice belonged to something that would eat him, nor that it was the voice of a ghost. But a new and different sort of trembling came over him. Yet he felt glad too.

The mist was turning from black to grey and from grey to white. This must have begun to happen some time ago, but while he had been talking to the Thing he had not been noticing anything else. Now, the whiteness around him became a shining whiteness; his eyes began to blink. Somewhere ahead he could hear birds singing. He knew the night was over at last. He could see the mane and ears and head of his horse quite easily now. A golden light fell on them from the left. He thought it was the sun.

He turned and saw, pacing beside him, taller than the horse, a Lion. The horse did not seem to be afraid of it or else could not see it. It was from the Lion that the light came. No one ever saw anything more terrible or beautiful.

Luckily Shasta had lived all his life too far south in Calormen to have heard the tales that were whispered in Tashbaan about a dreadful Narnian demon that appeared in the form of a lion. And of course he knew none of the true stories about Aslan, the great Lion, the son of the Emperor-over-sea, the King above all High Kings in Narnia. But after one glance at the Lion's face he slipped out of the saddle and fell at its feet. He couldn't say anything but then he didn't want to say anything, and he knew he needn't say anything.

The High King above all kings stooped towards him. Its mane, and some strange and solemn perfume that hung about the mane, was all round him. It touched his forehead with its tongue. He lifted his face and their eyes met. Then instantly the pale brightness of the mist and the fiery brightness of the Lion rolled themselves together into a swirling glory and gathered themselves up and disappeared. He was alone with the horse on a grassy hillside under a blue sky. And there were birds singing.

CHAPTER 12

SHASTA IN NARNIA

'WAS it all a dream?' wondered Shasta. But it couldn't have been a dream for there in the grass before him he saw the deep, large print of the Lion's front right paw. It took one's breath away to think of the weight that could make a footprint like that. But there was something more remarkable than the size about it. As he looked at it, water had already filled the bottom of it. Soon it was full to the brim, and then overflowing, and a little stream was running downhill, past him, over the grass.

Shasta stooped and drank – a very long drink – and then dipped his face in and splashed his head. It was extremely cold, and clear as glass, and refreshed him very much. After that he stood up, shaking the water out of his ears and flinging the wet hair back from his forehead, and began to take stock of his surroundings.

Apparently it was still very early morning. The sun had only just risen, and it had risen out of the forests which he saw low down and far away on his right. The country which he was looking at was absolutely new to him. It was a green valley-land dotted with trees through which he caught the gleam of a river that wound away roughly to the North-West. On the far side of the valley there were high and even rocky hills, but they were lower than the mountains he had seen yesterday. Then he began to guess where he was. He turned and looked behind him and saw that the slope on which he was standing belonged to a range of far higher mountains.

'I see,' said Shasta to himself. 'Those are the big mountains between Archenland and Narnia. I was on the other side of them yesterday. I must have come through the pass in the night. What luck that I hit it! – at least it wasn't luck at all really, it was *Him*. And now I'm in Narnia.'

He turned and unsaddled his horse and took off its bridle – 'Though you *are* a perfectly horrid horse,' he said. It took no notice of this remark and immediately began eating grass. That horse had a very low opinion of Shasta.

'I wish I could eat grass!' thought Shasta. 'It's no good going back to Anvard, it'll all be besieged. I'd better get lower down into the valley and see if I can get anything to eat.'

So he went on downhill (the thick dew was cruelly cold to his bare feet) till he came into a wood. There was a kind of track running through it and he had not followed this for many minutes when he heard a thick and rather wheezy voice saying to him,

'Good morning, neighbour.'

Shasta looked round eagerly to find the speaker and presently saw a small, prickly person with a dark face who had just come out from among the trees. At least, it was small for a person but very big indeed for a hedgehog, which was what it was.

'Good morning,' said Shasta. 'But I'm not a neighbour. In fact I'm a stranger in these parts.'

'Ah?' said the Hedgehog inquiringly.

'I've come over the mountains – from Archenland, you know.'

'Ah, Archenland,' said the Hedgehog. 'That's a terrible long way. Never been there myself.'

'And I think, perhaps,' said Shasta, 'someone ought to be told that there's an army of savage Calormenes attacking Anvard at this very moment.'

'You don't say so!' answered the Hedgehog. 'Well, think of that. And they do say that Calormen is hundreds and thousands of miles away, right at the world's end, across a great sea of sand.'

'It's not nearly as far as you think,' said Shasta. 'And oughtn't something to be done about this attack on Anvard. Oughtn't your High King to be told?'

'Certain sure, something ought to be done about it,' said the Hedgehog. 'But you see I'm just on my way to bed for a good day's sleep. Hullo, neighbour!'

The last words were addressed to an immense biscuit-coloured rabbit whose head had just popped up from somewhere beside the path. The Hedgehog immediately told the Rabbit what it had just learned from Shasta. The

Rabbit agreed that this was very remarkable news and
that somebody ought to tell someone about it with a view
to doing something.

And so it went on. Every few minutes they were joined
by other creatures, some from the branches overhead and
some from little underground houses at their feet, till the
party consisted of five rabbits, a squirrel, two magpies, a
goat-foot faun, and a mouse, who all talked at the same
time and all agreed with the Hedgehog. For the truth was
that in that golden age when the Witch and the Winter had
gone and Peter the High King ruled at Cair Paravel, the
smaller woodland people of Narnia were so safe and happy
that they were getting a little careless.

Presently, however, two more practical people arrived
in the little wood. One was a Red Dwarf whose name
appeared to be Duffle. The other was a stag, a beautiful
lordly creature with wide liquid eyes, dappled flanks and
legs so thin and graceful that they looked as if you could
break them with two fingers.

'Lion alive!' roared the Dwarf as soon as he had heard
the news. 'And if that's so, why are we all standing still,
chattering? Enemies at Anvard! News must be sent to
Cair Paravel at once. The army must be called out. Narnia
must go to the aid of King Lune.'

'Ah!' said the Hedgehog. 'But you won't find the High
King at the Cair. He's away to the North trouncing those
giants. And talking of giants, neighbours, that puts me in
mind—'

'Who'll take our message?' interrupted the Dwarf.
'Anyone here got more speed than me?'

'I've got speed,' said the Stag. 'What's my message?
How many Calormenes?'

'Two hundred: under Prince Rabadash. And –' But the Stag was already away – all four legs off the ground at once, and in a moment its white stern had disappeared among the remoter trees.

'Wonder where he's going,' said a Rabbit. 'He won't find the High King at Cair Paravel, you know.'

'He'll find Queen Lucy,' said Duffle. 'And then – hullo! What's wrong with the Human? It looks pretty green. Why, I do believe it's quite faint. Perhaps it's mortal hungry. When did you last have a meal, youngster?'

'Yesterday morning,' said Shasta weakly.

'Come on, then, come on,' said the Dwarf, at once throwing his thick little arms round Shasta's waist to support him. 'Why, neighbours, we ought all to be ashamed of ourselves! You come with me, lad. Breakfast! better than talking.'

With a great deal of bustle, muttering reproaches to itself, the Dwarf half led and half supported Shasta at a great speed further into the wood and a little downhill. It was a longer walk than Shasta wanted at that moment and his legs had begun to feel very shaky before they came out from the trees on to bare hillside. There they found a little house with a smoking chimney and an open door, and as they came to the doorway Duffle called out,

'Hey, brothers! A visitor for breakfast.'

And immediately, mixed with a sizzling sound, there came to Shasta a simply delightful smell. It was one he had never smelled in his life before, but I hope you have. It was, in fact, the smell of bacon and eggs and mushrooms all frying in a pan.

'Mind your head, lad,' said Duffle a moment too late,

for Shasta had already bashed his forehead against the low lintel of the door. 'Now,' continued the Dwarf, 'sit you down. The table's a bit low for you, but then the stool's low too. That's right. And here's porridge – and here's a jug of cream – and here's a spoon.'

By the time Shasta had finished his porridge, the Dwarf's two brothers (whose names were Rogin and Bricklethumb) were putting the dish of bacon and eggs and mushrooms, and the coffee pot and the hot milk, and the toast, on the table.

It was all new and wonderful to Shasta for Calormene food is quite different. He didn't even know what the slices of brown stuff were, for he had never seen toast before. He didn't know what the yellow soft thing they smeared on the toast was, because in Calormen you nearly always get oil instead of butter. And the house itself was quite different from the dark, frowsty, fish-smelling hut of Arsheesh and from the pillared and carpeted halls in the palaces of Tashbaan. The roof was very low, and everything was made of wood, and there was a cuckoo-clock and a red-and-white checked table-cloth and a bowl of wild flowers and little white curtains on the thick-paned windows. It was also rather troublesome having to use dwarf cups and plates and knives and forks. This meant that helpings were very small, but then there were a great many helpings, so that Shasta's plate or cup was being filled every moment, and every moment the Dwarfs themselves were saying, 'Butter please', or 'Another cup of coffee,' or 'I'd like a few more mushrooms,' or 'What about frying another egg or so?' And when at last they had all eaten as much as they possibly could the three Dwarfs drew lots for who would do the washing-up, and

Rogin was the unlucky one. Then Duffle and Brickle-thumb took Shasta outside to a bench which ran against the cottage wall, and they all stretched out their legs and gave a great sigh of contentment and the two Dwarfs lit their pipes. The dew was off the grass now and the sun was warm; indeed, if there hadn't been a light breeze, it would have been too hot.

'Now, Stranger,' said Duffle, 'I'll show you the lie of the land. You can see nearly all South Narnia from here, and we're rather proud of the view. Right away on your left, beyond those near hills, you can just see the Western Mountains. And that round hill away on your right is called the Hill of the Stone Table. Just beyond–'

But at that moment he was interrupted by a snore from Shasta who, what with his night's journey and his excellent breakfast, had gone fast asleep. The kindly Dwarfs, as soon as they noticed this, began making signs to each other not to wake him, and indeed did so much whispering and nodding and getting up and tiptoeing away that they certainly would have waked him if he had been less tired.

He slept pretty well nearly all day but woke up in time for supper. The beds in that house were all too small for him but they made him a fine bed of heather on the floor, and he never stirred nor dreamed all night. Next morning they had just finished breakfast when they heard a shrill, exciting sound from outside.

'Trumpets!' said all the Dwarfs, as they and Shasta all came running out.

The trumpets sounded again: a new noise to Shasta, not huge and solemn like the horns of Tashbaan nor gay and merry like King Lune's hunting horn, but clear and sharp and valiant. The noise was coming from the woods to the

East, and soon there was a noise of horse-hoofs mixed with it. A moment later the head of the column came into sight.

First came the Lord Peridan on a bay horse carrying the great banner of Narnia – a red lion on a green ground. Shasta knew him at once. Then came three people riding abreast, two on great chargers and one on a pony. The two on the chargers were King Edmund and a fair-haired lady with a very merry face who wore a helmet and mail shirt and carried a bow across her shoulder and a quiver full of arrows at her side. ('The Queen Lucy,' whispered Duffle.) But the one on the pony was Corin. After that came the main body of the army: men on ordinary horses, men on Talking Horses (who didn't mind being ridden on proper occasions, as when Narnia went to war), centaurs, stern, hard-bitten bears, great Talking Dogs, and last of all six giants. For there are good giants in Narnia. But though he knew they were on the right side Shasta at first could hardly bear to look at them; there are some things that take a lot of getting used to.

Just as the King and Queen reached the cottage and the Dwarfs began making low bows to them, King Edmund called out,

'Now, friends! Time for a halt and a morsel!' and at once there was a great bustle of people dismounting and haversacks being opened and conversation beginning when Corin came running up to Shasta and seized both his hands and cried,

'What! *You* here! So you got through all right? I *am* glad. Now we shall have some sport. And isn't it luck! We only got into harbour at Cair Paravel yesterday morning and the very first person who met us was Chervy the

Stag with all this news of an attack on Anvard. Don't you
think –'

'Who is your Highness's friend?' said King Edmund
who had just got off his horse.

'Don't you see, Sire?' said Corin. 'It's my double: the
boy you mistook me for at Tashbaan.'

'Why, so he is your double,' exclaimed Queen Lucy. 'As
like as two twins. This is a marvellous thing.'

'Please, your Majesty,' said Shasta to King Edmund, 'I
was no traitor, really I wasn't. And I couldn't help hearing
your plans. But I'd never have dreamed of telling them to
your enemies.'

'I know now that you were no traitor, boy,' said King
Edmund, laying his hand on Shasta's head. 'But if you
would not be taken for one, another time try not to hear
what's meant for other ears. But all's well.'

After that there was so much bustle and talk and coming
and going that Shasta for a few minutes lost sight of Corin

and Edmund and Lucy. But Corin was the sort of boy whom one is sure to hear of pretty soon and it wasn't very long before Shasta heard King Edmund saying in a loud voice:

'By the Lion's Mane, prince, this is too much! Will your Highness never be better? You are more of a heart's-scald than our whole army together! I'd as lief have a regiment of hornets in my command as you.'

Shasta wormed his way through the crowd and there saw Edmund, looking very angry indeed, Corin looking a little ashamed of himself, and a strange Dwarf sitting on the ground making faces. A couple of fauns had apparently just been helping it out of its armour.

'If I had but my cordial with me,' Queen Lucy was saying, 'I could soon mend this. But the High King has so strictly charged me not to carry it commonly to the wars and to keep it only for great extremities!'

What had happened was this. As soon as Corin had

spoken to Shasta, Corin's elbow had been plucked by a Dwarf in the army called Thornbut.

'What is it, Thornbut?' Corin had said.

'Your Royal Highness,' said Thornbut, drawing him aside, 'our march today will bring us through the pass and right to your royal father's castle. We may be in battle before night.'

'I know,' said Corin. 'Isn't it splendid!'

'Splendid or not,' said Thornbut, 'I have the strictest orders from King Edmund to see to it that your Highness is not in the fight. You will be allowed to see it, and that's treat enough for your Highness's little years.'

'Oh what nonsense!' Corin burst out. 'Of course I'm going to fight. Why, the Queen Lucy's going to be with the archers.'

'The Queen's grace will do as she pleases,' said Thornbut. 'But you are in my charge. Either I must have your solemn and princely word that you'll keep your pony beside mine – not half a neck ahead – till I give your Highness leave to depart: or else – it is his Majesty's word – we must go with our wrists tied together like two prisoners.'

'I'll knock you down if you try to bind me,' said Corin.

'I'd like to see your Highness do it,' said the Dwarf.

That was quite enough for a boy like Corin and in a second he and the Dwarf were at it hammer and tongs. It would have been an even match for, though Corin had longer arms and more height, the Dwarf was older and tougher. But it was never fought out (that's the worst of fights on a rough hillside) for by very bad luck Thornbut trod on a loose stone, came flat down on his nose, and found when he tried to get up that he had sprained his ankle: a real excruciating sprain which would keep him from walking or riding for at least a fortnight.

'See what your Highness has done,' said King Edmund. 'Deprived us of a proved warrior on the very edge of battle.'

'I'll take his place, Sire,' said Corin.

'Pshaw,' said Edmund. 'No one doubts your courage. But a boy in battle is a danger only to his own side.'

At that moment the King was called away to attend to something else, and Corin, after apologizing handsomely to the Dwarf, rushed up to Shasta and whispered,

'Quick. There's a spare pony now, and the Dwarf's armour. Put it on before anyone notices.'

'What for?' said Shasta.

'Why, so that you and I can fight in the battle of course! Don't you want to?'

'Oh – ah, yes, of course,' said Shasta. But he hadn't been thinking of doing so at all, and began to get a most uncomfortable prickly feeling in his spine.

'That's right,' said Corin. 'Over your head. Now the sword-belt. But we must ride near the tail of the column and keep as quiet as mice. Once the battle begins everyone will be far too busy to notice us.'

CHAPTER 13

THE FIGHT AT ANVARD

By about eleven o'clock the whole company was once more on the march, riding westward with the mountains on their left. Corin and Shasta rode right at the rear with the Giants immediately in front of them. Lucy and Edmund and Peridan were busy with their plans for the battle and though Lucy once said, 'But where is his goosecap Highness?' Edmund only replied, 'Not in the front, and that's good news enough. Leave well alone.'

Shasta told Corin most of his adventures and explained that he had learned all his riding from a horse and didn't really know how to use the reins. Corin instructed him in this, besides telling him all about their secret sailing from Tashbaan.

'And where is the Queen Susan?'

'At Cair Paravel,' said Corin. 'She's not like Lucy, you know, who's as good as a man, or at any rate as good as a boy. Queen Susan is more like an ordinary grown-up lady. She doesn't ride to the wars, though she is an excellent archer.'

The hillside path which they were following became narrower all the time and the drop on their right hand became steeper. At last they were going in single file along the edge of a precipice and Shasta shuddered to think that he had done the same last night without knowing it. 'But of course,' he thought, 'I was quite safe. That is why the Lion kept on my left. He was between me and the edge all the time.'

Then the path went left and south away from the cliff and there were thick woods on both sides of it and they went steeply up and up into the pass. There would have been a splendid view from the top if it were open ground but among all those trees you could see nothing – only, every now and then, some huge pinnacle of rock above the tree-tops, and an eagle or two wheeling high up in the blue air.

'They smell battle,' said Corin, pointing at the birds. 'They know we're preparing a feed for them.'

Shasta didn't like this at all.

When they had crossed the neck of the pass and come a good deal lower they reached more open ground and from here Shasta could see all Archenland, blue and hazy, spread out below him and even (he thought) a hint of the desert beyond it. But the sun, which had perhaps two hours or so to go before it set, was in his eyes and he couldn't make things out distinctly.

Here the army halted and spread out in a line, and there was a great deal of rearranging. A whole detachment of very dangerous-looking Talking Beasts whom Shasta had not noticed before and who were mostly of the cat kind (leopards, panthers, and the like) went padding and growling to take up their positions on the left. The giants were ordered to the right, and before going there they all took off something they had been carrying on their backs and sat down for a moment. Then Shasta saw that what they had been carrying and were now putting on were pairs of boots: horrid, heavy, spiked boots which came up to their knees. Then they sloped their huge clubs over their shoulders and marched to their battle position. The archers, with Queen Lucy, fell to the rear and you could first see them bending their bows and then hear the twang-twang as they tested the strings. And wherever you looked you could see people tightening girths, putting on helmets, drawing swords, and throwing cloaks to the ground. There was hardly any talking now. It was very solemn and very dreadful. 'I'm in for it now – I really am in for it now,' thought Shasta.

Then there came noises far ahead: the sound of many men shouting and a steady thud-thud-thud.

'Battering ram,' whispered Corin. 'They're battering the gate.'

Even Corin looked quite serious now.

'Why doesn't King Edmund get *on*?' he said. 'I can't stand this waiting about. Chilly too.'

Shasta nodded: hoping he didn't look as frightened as he felt.

The trumpet at last! On the move now – now trotting – the banner streaming out in the wind. They had topped a low ridge now, and below them the whole scene suddenly opened out; a little, many-towered castle with its gate towards them. No moat, unfortunately, but of course the gate shut and the portcullis down. On the walls they could see, like little white dots, the faces of the defenders. Down below, about fifty of the Calormenes, dismounted, were steadily swinging a great tree trunk against the gate. But at once the scene changed. The main bulk of Rabadash's men had been on foot ready to assault the gate. But now he had seen the Narnians sweeping down from the ridge. There is no doubt those Calormenes are wonderfully trained. It seemed to Shasta only a second before a whole line of the enemy were on horseback again, wheeling round to meet them, swinging towards them.

And now a gallop. The ground between the two armies grew less every moment. Faster, faster. All swords out now, all shields up to the nose, all prayers said, all teeth clenched. Shasta was dreadfully frightened. But it suddenly came into his head, 'If you funk this, you'll funk every battle all your life. Now or never.'

But when at last the two lines met he had really very little idea of what happened. There was a frightful confusion and an appalling noise. His sword was knocked clean out of his hand pretty soon. And he'd got the reins tangled somehow. Then he found himself slipping. Then a spear came straight at him and as he ducked to avoid it he rolled right off his horse, bashed his left knuckles terribly against someone else's armour, and then –

But it is no use trying to describe the battle from Shasta's point of view; he understood too little of the fight in general and even of his own part in it. The best way I can tell you what really happened is to take you some miles away to where the Hermit of the Southern March sat gazing into the smooth pool beneath the spreading tree, with Bree and Hwin and Aravis beside him.

For it was in this pool that the Hermit looked when he

wanted to know what was going on in the world outside
the green walls of his hermitage. There, as in a mirror, he
could see, at certain times, what was going on in the streets
of cities far farther south than Tashbaan, or what ships
were putting into Redhaven in the remote Seven Isles,
or what robbers or wild beasts stirred in the great Western
forests between Lantern Waste and Telmar. And all this
day he had hardly left his pool, even to eat or drink, for he
knew that great events were on foot in Archenland. Aravis
and the Horses gazed into it too. They could see it was a
magic pool: instead of reflecting the tree and the sky it
revealed cloudy and coloured shapes moving, always
moving, in its depths. But they could see nothing clearly.
The Hermit could and from time to time he told them what
he saw. A little while before Shasta rode into his first battle,
the Hermit had begun speaking like this:

'I see one – two – three eagles wheeling in the gap by
Stormness Head. One is the oldest of all the eagles. He
would not be out unless battle was at hand. I see him wheel
to and fro, peering down sometimes at Anvard and sometimes to the east, behind Stormness. Ah – I see now what
Rabadash and his men have been so busy at all day. They
have felled and lopped a great tree and they are now coming out of the woods carrying it as a ram. They have
learned something from the failure of last night's assault.
He would have been wiser if he had set his men to making
ladders: but it takes longer and he is impatient. Fool that
he is! he ought to have ridden back to Tashbaan as soon as
the first attack failed, for his whole plan depended on
speed and surprise. Now they are bringing their ram into
position. King Lune's men are shooting hard from the
walls. Five Calormenes have fallen: but not many will.

They have their shields above their heads. Rabadash is
giving his orders now. With him are his most trusted lords,
fierce Tarkaans from the eastern provinces. I can see their
faces. There is Corradin of Castle Tormunt, and Azrooh,
and Chlamash, and Ilgamuth of the twisted lip, and a tall
Tarkaan with a crimson beard –'

'By the Mane, my old master Anradin!' said Bree.

'S-s-sh,' said Aravis.

'Now the ram has started. If I could hear as well as see,
what a noise that would make! Stroke after stroke: and no
gate can stand it for ever. But wait! Something up by
Stormness has scared the birds. They're coming out in
masses. And wait again . . . I can't see yet . . . ah! Now I
can. The whole ridge, up on the east, is black with horsemen. If only the wind would catch that standard and spread
it out. They're over the ridge now, whoever they are.
Aha! I've seen the banner now. Narnia, Narnia! It's the
red lion. They're in full career down the hill now. I can see
King Edmund. There's a woman behind among the
archers. Oh! –'

'What is it?' asked Hwin breathlessly.

'All his Cats are dashing out from the left of the line.'

'Cats?' said Aravis.

'Great cats, leopards and such,' said the Hermit impatiently. 'I see, I see. The Cats are coming round in a
circle to get at the horses of the dismounted men. A good
stroke. The Calormene horses are mad with terror already.
Now the Cats are in among them. But Rabadash has
re-formed his line and has a hundred men in the saddle.
They're riding to meet the Narnians. There's only a hundred yards between the two lines now. Only fifty. I can
see King Edmund, I can see the Lord Peridan. There are

two mere children in the Narnian line. What can the King be about to let them into the battle? Only ten yards – the lines have met. The Giants on the Narnian right are doing wonders . . . but one's down . . . shot through the eye, I suppose. The centre's all in a muddle. I can see more on the left. There are the two boys again. Lion alive! one is Prince Corin. The other, like him as two peas. It's your little Shasta. Corin is fighting like a man. He's killed a Calormene. I can see a bit of the centre now. Rabadash and Edmund almost met then, but the press has separated them –'

'What about Shasta?' said Aravis.

'Oh the fool!' groaned the Hermit. 'Poor, brave little fool. He knows nothing about this work. He's making no use at all of his shield. His whole side's exposed. He hasn't the faintest idea what to do with his sword. Oh, he's remembered it now. He's waving it wildly about . . . nearly cut his own pony's head off, and he will in a moment if he's not careful. It's been knocked out of his hand now. It's mere murder sending a child into the battle; he can't live five minutes. Duck, you fool – oh, he's down.'

'Killed?' asked three voices breathlessly.

'How can I tell?' said the Hermit. 'The Cats have done their work. All the riderless horses are dead or escaped now: no retreat for the Calormenes on *them*. Now the Cats are turning back into the main battle. They're leaping on the rams-men. The ram is down. Oh, good! good! The gates are opening from the inside: there's going to be a sortie. The first three are out. It's King Lune in the middle: the brothers Dar and Darrin on each side of him. Behind them are Tran and Shar and Cole with his brother Colin. There are ten – twenty – nearly thirty of them out by now.

The Calormene line is being forced back upon them. King Edmund is dealing marvellous strokes. He's just slashed Corradin's head off. Lots of Calormenes have thrown down their arms and are running for the woods. Those that remain are hard pressed. The Giants are closing in on the right – Cats on the left – King Lune from their rear. The Calormenes are a little knot now, fighting back to back. Your Tarkaan's down, Bree. Lune and Azrooh are fighting hand to hand; the King looks like winning – the King is keeping it up well – the King has won. Azrooh's down. King Edmund's down – no, he's up again: he's at it with Rabadash. They're fighting in the very gate of the castle. Several Calormenes have surrendered. Darrin has killed Ilgamuth. I can't see what's happened to Rabadash. I think he's dead, leaning against the castle wall, but I don't know. Chlamash and King Edmund are still fighting but the battle is over everywhere else. Chlamash has surrendered. The battle *is* over. The Calormenes are utterly defeated.'

When Shasta fell off his horse he gave himself up for lost. But horses, even in a battle, tread on human beings very much less than you would suppose. After a very horrible ten minutes or so Shasta realized suddenly that there were no longer any horses stamping about in the immediate neighbourhood and that the noise (for there were still a good many noises going on) was no longer that of a battle. He sat up and stared about him. Even he, little as he knew of battles, could soon see that the Archenlanders and Narnians had won. The only living Calormenes he could see were prisoners, the castle gates were wide open, and King Lune and King Edmund were shaking hands across the battering ram. From the circle of lords and warriors around them there arose a sound of breathless and excited, but obviously cheerful, conversation. And then, suddenly, it all united and swelled into a great roar of laughter.

Shasta picked himself up, feeling uncommonly stiff, and ran towards the sound to see what the joke was. A very curious sight met his eyes. The unfortunate Rabadash appeared to be suspended from the castle walls. His feet,

which were about two feet from the ground, were kicking wildly. His chain-shirt was somehow hitched up so that it was horribly tight under the arms and came half way over his face. In fact he looked just as a man looks if you catch him in the very act of getting into a stiff shirt that is a little too small for him. As far as could be made out afterwards (and you may be sure the story was well talked over for many a day) what had happened was something like this. Early in the battle one of the Giants had made an unsuccessful stamp at Rabadash with his spiked boot: unsuccessful because it didn't crush Rabadash, which was what the Giant had intended, but not quite useless because one of the spikes tore the chain mail, just as you or I might tear an ordinary shirt. So Rabadash, by the time he encountered Edmund at the gate, had a hole in the back of his hauberk. And when Edmund pressed him back nearer and nearer to the wall, he jumped up on a mounting block and stood there raining down blows on Edmund from above. But then, finding that this position, by raising him above the heads of everyone else, made him a mark for every arrow from the Narnian bows, he decided to jump down again. And he meant to look and sound – no doubt for a moment he *did* look and sound – very grand and very dreadful as he jumped, crying, 'The bolt of Tash falls from above.' But he had to jump sideways because the crowd in front of him left him no landing place in that direction. And then, in the neatest way you could wish, the tear in the back of his hauberk caught on a hook in the wall. (Ages ago this hook had had a ring in it for tying horses to.) And there he found himself, like a piece of washing hung up to dry, with everyone laughing at him.

'Let me down, Edmund,' howled Rabadash. 'Let me down and fight me like a king and a man; or if you are too great a coward to do that, kill me at once.'

'Certainly,' began King Edmund, but King Lune interrupted.

'By your Majesty's good leave,' said King Lune to Edmund. 'Not so.' Then turning to Rabadash he said, 'Your royal Highness, if you had given that challenge a week ago, I'll answer for it there was no one in King Edmund's dominion, from the High King down to the smallest Talking Mouse, who would have refused it. But by attacking our castle of Anvard in time of peace without defiance sent, you have proved yourself no knight, but a traitor, and one rather to be whipped by the hangman than to be suffered to cross swords with any person of honour. Take him down, bind him, and carry him within till our pleasure is further known.'

Strong hands wrenched Rabadash's sword from him and he was carried away into the castle, shouting, threatening, cursing, and even crying. For though he could have faced torture he couldn't bear being made ridiculous. In Tashbaan everyone had always taken him seriously.

At that moment Corin ran up to Shasta, seized his hand and started dragging him towards King Lune. 'Here he is, Father, here he is,' cried Corin.

'Aye, and here *thou* art, at last,' said the King in a very gruff voice. 'And hast been in the battle, clean contrary to your obedience. A boy to break a father's heart! At your age a rod to your breech were fitter than a sword in your fist, ha!' But everyone, including Corin, could see that the King was very proud of him.

'Chide him no more, Sire, if it please you,' said Lord

Darrin. 'His Highness would not be your son if he did not inherit your conditions. It would grieve your Majesty more if he had to be reproved for the opposite fault.'

'Well, well,' grumbled the King. 'We'll pass it over for this time. And now – '

What came next surprised Shasta as much as anything that had ever happened to him in his life. He found himself suddenly embraced in a bear-like hug by King Lune and kissed on both cheeks. Then the King set him down again and said, 'Stand here together, boys, and let all the court see you. Hold up your heads. Now, gentlemen, look on them both. Has any man any doubts?'

And still Shasta could not understand why everyone stared at him and at Corin nor what all the cheering was about.

CHAPTER 14

HOW BREE BECAME A WISER HORSE

WE must now return to Aravis and the Horses. The Hermit, watching his pool, was able to tell them that Shasta was not killed or even seriously wounded, for he saw him get up and saw how affectionately he was greeted by King Lune. But as he could only see, not hear, he did not know what anyone was saying and, once the fighting had stopped and the talking had begun, it was not worth while looking in the pool any longer.

Next morning, while the Hermit was indoors, the three of them discussed what they should do next.

'I've had enough of this,' said Hwin. 'The Hermit has been very good to us and I'm very much obliged to him I'm sure. But I'm getting as fat as a pet pony, eating all day and getting no exercise. Let's go on to Narnia.'

'Oh not today, Ma'am,' said Bree. 'I wouldn't hurry things. Some other day, don't you think?'

'We must see Shasta first and say good-bye to him – and – and apologize,' said Aravis.

'Exactly!' said Bree with great enthusiasm. 'Just what I was going to say.'

'Oh, of course,' said Hwin. 'I expect he is in Anvard. Naturally we'd look in on him and say good-bye. But that's on our way. And why shouldn't we start at once? After all, I thought it was Narnia we all wanted to get to?'

'I suppose so,' said Aravis. She was beginning to wonder

what exactly she would do when she got there and was feeling a little lonely.

'Of course, of course,' said Bree hastily. 'But there's no need to rush things, if you know what I mean.'

'No, I don't know what you mean,' said Hwin. 'Why don't you want to go?'

'M-m-m, broo-hoo,' muttered Bree. 'Well, don't you see, Ma'am – it's an important occasion – returning to one's own country – entering society – the best society – it is so essential to make a good impression – not perhaps looking quite ourselves, yet, eh?'

Hwin broke out into a horse-laugh. 'It's your tail, Bree! I see it all now. You want to wait till your tail's grown again! And we don't even know if tails are worn long in Narnia. Really, Bree, you're as vain as that Tarkheena in Tashbaan!'

'You *are* silly, Bree,' said Aravis.

'By the Lion's Mane, Tarkheena, I'm nothing of the sort,' said Bree indignantly. 'I have a proper respect for myself and for my fellow horses, that's all.'

'Bree,' said Aravis, who was not very interested in the cut of his tail, 'I've been wanting to ask you something for a long time. Why do you keep on swearing *By the Lion* and *By the Lion's Mane*? I thought you hated lions.'

'So I do,' answered Bree. 'But when I speak of *the* Lion of course I mean Aslan, the great deliverer of Narnia who drove away the Witch and the Winter. All Narnians swear by *him*.'

'But is he a lion?'

'No, no, of course not,' said Bree in a rather shocked voice.

'All the stories about him in Tashbaan say he is,' replied

Aravis. 'And if he isn't a lion why do you call him a lion?'

'Well, you'd hardly understand that at your age,' said Bree. 'And I was only a little foal when I left so I don't quite fully understand it myself.'

(Bree was standing with his back to the green wall while he said this, and the other two were facing him. He was talking in rather a superior tone with his eyes half shut; that was why he didn't see the changed expression in the faces of Hwin and Aravis. They had good reason to have open mouths and staring eyes; because while Bree spoke they saw an enormous lion leap up from outside and balance itself on the top of the green wall; only it was a brighter yellow and it was bigger and more beautiful and more alarming than any lion they had ever seen. And at once it jumped down inside the wall and began approaching Bree from behind. It made no noise at all. And Hwin and Aravis couldn't make any noise themselves, no more than if they were frozen.)

'No doubt,' continued Bree, 'when they speak of him as a Lion they only mean he's as strong as a lion or (to our enemies, of course) as fierce as a lion. Or something of that kind. Even a little girl like you, Aravis, must see that it would be quite absurd to suppose he is a *real* lion. Indeed it would be disrespectful. If he was a lion he'd have to be a Beast just like the rest of us. Why!' (and here Bree began to laugh) 'If he was a lion he'd have four paws, and a tail, and *Whiskers*! . . . Aie, ooh, hoo-hoo! Help!'

For just as he said the word *Whiskers* one of Aslan's had actually tickled his ear. Bree shot away like an arrow to the other side of the enclosure and there turned; the wall was too high for him to jump and he could fly no farther.

Aravis and Hwin both started back. There was about a second of intense silence.

Then Hwin, though shaking all over, gave a strange little neigh, and trotted across to the Lion.

'Please,' she said, 'you're so beautiful. You may eat me if you like. I'd sooner be eaten by you than fed by anyone else.'

'Dearest daughter,' said Aslan, planting a lion's kiss on her twitching, velvet nose, 'I knew you would not be long in coming to me. Joy shall be yours.'

Then he lifted his head and spoke in a louder voice.

'Now, Bree,' he said, 'you poor, proud, frightened Horse, draw near. Nearer still, my son. Do not dare not to dare. Touch me. Smell me. Here are my paws, here is my tail, these are my whiskers. I am a true Beast.'

'Aslan,' said Bree in a shaken voice, 'I'm afraid I must be rather a fool.'

'Happy the Horse who knows that while he is still young. Or the Human either. Draw near, Aravis my daughter. See! My paws are velveted. You will not be torn this time.'

'This time, sir?' said Aravis.

'It was I who wounded you,' said Aslan. 'I am the only lion you met in all your journeyings. Do you know why I tore you?'

'No, sir.'

'The scratches on your back, tear for tear, throb for throb, blood for blood, were equal to the stripes laid on the back of your stepmother's slave because of the drugged sleep you cast upon her. You needed to know what it felt like.'

'Yes, sir. Please –'

'Ask on, my dear,' said Aslan.

'Will any more harm come to her by what I did?'

'Child,' said the Lion, 'I am telling you your story, not hers. No one is told any story but their own.' Then he shook his head and spoke in a lighter voice.

'Be merry, little ones,' he said. 'We shall meet soon again. But before that you will have another visitor.' Then in one bound he reached the top of the wall and vanished from their sight.

Strange to say, they felt no inclination to talk to one another about him after he had gone. They all moved slowly away to different parts of the quiet grass and there paced to and fro, each alone, thinking.

About half an hour later the two Horses were summoned to the back of the house to eat something nice that the Hermit had got ready for them and Aravis, still walking and thinking, was startled by the harsh sound of a trumpet outside the gate.

'Who is there?' said Aravis.

'His Royal Highness Prince Cor of Archenland,' said a voice from outside.

Aravis undid the door and opened it, drawing back a little way to let the strangers in.

Two soldiers with halberds came first and took their stand at each side of the entry. Then followed a herald, and the trumpeter.

'His Royal Highness Prince Cor of Archenland desires an audience of the Lady Aravis,' said the Herald. Then he and the trumpeter drew aside and bowed and the soldiers saluted and the Prince himself came in. All his attendants withdrew and closed the gate behind them.

The Prince bowed, and a very clumsy bow for a Prince

it was. Aravis curtsied in the Calormene style (which is not at all like ours) and did it very well because, of course, she had been taught how. Then she looked up and saw what sort of person this Prince was.

She saw a mere boy. He was bare-headed and his fair hair was encircled with a very thin band of gold, hardly

thicker than a wire. His upper tunic was of white cambric, as fine as a handkerchief, so that the bright red tunic beneath it showed through. His left hand, which rested on his enamelled sword hilt, was bandaged.

Aravis looked twice at his face before she gasped and said, 'Why! It's Shasta!'

Shasta all at once turned very red and began speaking very quickly. 'Look here, Aravis,' he said, 'I do hope you won't think I'm got up like this (and the trumpeter and all) to try to impress you or make out that I'm different or any

rot of that sort. Because I'd far rather have come in my
old clothes, but they're burnt now, and my father said –'

'Your father?' said Aravis.

'Apparently King Lune is my father,' said Shasta. 'I
might really have guessed it. Corin being so like me. We
were twins, you see. Oh, and my name isn't Shasta, it's
Cor.'

'Cor is a nicer name than Shasta,' said Aravis.

'Brothers' names run like that in Archenland,' said
Shasta (or Prince Cor as we must now call him). 'Like Dar
and Darrin, Cole and Colin and so on.'

'Shasta – I mean Cor,' said Aravis. 'No, shut up. There's
something I've got to say at once. I'm sorry I've been such
a pig. But I did change before I knew you were a Prince,
honestly I did: when you went back, and faced the Lion.'

'It wasn't really going to kill you at all, that Lion,' said
Cor.

'I know,' said Aravis, nodding. Both were still and
solemn for a moment as each saw that the other knew about
Aslan.

Suddenly Aravis remembered Cor's bandaged hand. 'I
say!' she cried, 'I forgot! You've been in a battle. Is that
a wound?'

'A mere scratch,' said Cor, using for the first time a
rather lordly tone. But a moment later he burst out laughing and said, 'If you want to know the truth, it isn't a
proper wound at all. I only took the skin off my knuckles
just as any clumsy fool might do without going near a
battle.'

'Still you were in the battle,' said Aravis. 'It must have
been wonderful.'

'It wasn't at all like what I thought,' said Cor.

'But Sha – Cor, I mean – you haven't told me anything yet about King Lune and how he found out who you were.'

'Well, let's sit down,' said Cor. 'For it's rather a long story. And by the way, Father's an absolute brick. I'd be just as pleased – or very nearly – at finding he's my father even if he wasn't a king. Even though Education and all sorts of horrible things are going to happen to me. But you want the story. Well, Corin and I were twins. And about a week after we were both born, apparently, they took us to a wise old Centaur in Narnia to be blessed or something. Now this Centaur was a prophet as a good many Centaurs are. Perhaps you haven't seen any Centaurs yet? There were some in the battle yesterday. Most remarkable people, but I can't say I feel quite at home with them yet. I say, Aravis, there are going to be a lot of things to get used to in these Northern countries.'

'Yes, there are,' said Aravis. 'But get on with the story.'

'Well, as soon as he saw Corin and me, it seems this Centaur looked at me and said, A day will come when that boy will save Archenland from the deadliest danger in which ever she lay. So of course my Father and Mother were very pleased. But there was someone present who wasn't. This was a chap called the Lord Bar who had been Father's Lord Chancellor. And apparently he'd done something wrong – *bezzling* or some word like that – I

didn't understand that part very well – and Father had had
to dismiss him. But nothing else was done to him and he
was allowed to go on living in Archenland. But he must
have been as bad as he could be, for it came out afterwards
he had been in the pay of the Tisroc and had sent a lot of
secret information to Tashbaan. So as soon as he heard I
was going to save Archenland from a great danger he
decided I must be put out of the way. Well, he succeeded
in kidnapping me (I don't exactly know how) and rode
away down the Winding Arrow to the coast. He'd had
everything prepared and there was a ship manned with his
own followers lying ready for him and he put out to sea
with me on board. But Father got wind of it, though not
quite in time, and was after him as quickly as he could.
The Lord Bar was already at sea when Father reached the
coast, but not out of sight. And Father was embarked in
one of his own warships within twenty minutes.

'It must have been a wonderful chase. They were six
days following Bar's galleon and brought her to battle on
the seventh. It was a great sea-fight (I heard a lot about it
yesterday evening) from ten o'clock in the morning till
sunset. Our people took the ship in the end. But I wasn't
there. The Lord Bar himself had been killed in the battle.
But one of his men said that, early that morning, as soon
as he saw he was certain to be overhauled, Bar had given
me to one of his knights and sent us both away in the ship's
boat. And that boat was never seen again. But of course
that was the same boat that Aslan (he seems to be at the
back of all the stories) pushed ashore at the right place for
Arsheesh to pick me up. I wish I knew that knight's name,
for he must have kept me alive and starved himself to do
it.'

'I suppose Aslan would say that was part of someone else's story,' said Aravis.

'I was forgetting that,' said Cor.

'And I wonder how the prophecy will work out,' said Aravis, 'and what the great danger is that you're to save Archenland from.'

'Well,' said Cor rather awkwardly, 'they seem to think I've done it already.'

Aravis clapped her hands. 'Why, of course!' she said. 'How stupid I am. And how wonderful! Archenland can never be in much greater danger than it was when Rabadash had crossed the Arrow with his two hundred horse and you hadn't yet got through with your message. Don't you feel proud?'

'I think I feel a bit scared,' said Cor.

'And you'll be living at Anvard now,' said Aravis rather wistfully.

'Oh!' said Cor, 'I'd nearly forgotten what I came about. Father wants you to come and live with us. He says there's been no lady in the court (they call it the court, I don't know why) since Mother died. Do, Aravis. You'll like Father – and Corin. They're not like me; they've been properly brought up. You needn't be afraid that – '

'Oh stop it,' said Aravis, 'or we'll have a real fight. Of course I'll come.'

'Now let's go and see the Horses,' said Cor.

There was a great and joyous meeting between Bree and Cor, and Bree, who was still in a rather subdued frame of mind, agreed to set out for Anvard at once: he and Hwin would cross into Narnia on the following day. All four bade an affectionate farewell to the Hermit and promised that they would soon visit him again. By about the middle of the morning they were on their way. The Horses had expected that Aravis and Cor would ride, but Cor explained that except in war, where everyone must do what he can do best, no one in Narnia or Archenland ever dreamed of mounting a Talking Horse.

This reminded poor Bree again of how little he knew about Narnian customs and what dreadful mistakes he might make. So while Hwin strolled along in a happy dream, Bree got more nervous and more self-conscious with every step he took.

'Buck up, Bree,' said Cor. 'It's far worse for me than for you. You aren't going to be *educated*. I shall be learning reading and writing and heraldry and dancing and history and music while you'll be galloping and rolling on the hills of Narnia to your heart's content.'

'But that's just the point,' groaned Bree. '*Do* Talking Horses roll? Supposing they don't? I can't bear to give it up. What do you think, Hwin?'

'I'm going to roll anyway,' said Hwin. 'I don't suppose any of them will care two lumps of sugar whether you roll or not.'

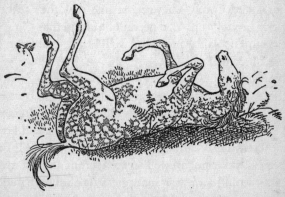

'Are we near that castle?' said Bree to Cor.

'Round the next bend,' said the Prince.

'Well,' said Bree, 'I'm going to have a good one now: it may be the last. Wait for me a minute.'

It was five minutes before he rose again, blowing hard and covered with bits of bracken.

'Now I'm ready,' he said in a voice of profound gloom. 'Lead on, Prince Cor, Narnia and the North.'

But he looked more like a horse going to a funeral than a long-lost captive returning to home and freedom.

CHAPTER 15

RABADASH THE RIDICULOUS

THE next turn of the road brought them out from among the trees and there, across green lawns, sheltered from the north wind by the high wooded ridge at its back, they saw the castle of Anvard. It was very old and built of a warm, reddish-brown stone.

Before they had reached the gate King Lune came out to meet them, not looking at all like Aravis's idea of a king and wearing the oldest of old clothes; for he had just come from making a round of the kennels with his Huntsman and had only stopped for a moment to wash his doggy hands. But the bow with which he greeted Aravis as he took her hand would have been stately enough for an Emperor.

'Little lady,' he said, 'we bid you very heartily welcome. If my dear wife were still alive we could make you better cheer but could not do it with a better will. And I am sorry that you have had misfortunes and been driven from your father's house, which cannot but be a grief to you. My son Cor has told me about your adventures together and all your valour.'

'It was he who did all that, Sir,' said Aravis. 'Why, he rushed at a lion to save me.'

'Eh, what's that?' said King Lune, his face brightening. 'I haven't heard that part of the story.'

Then Aravis told it. And Cor, who had very much wanted the story to be known, though he felt he couldn't tell it himself, didn't enjoy it so much as he had expected,

and indeed felt rather foolish. But his father enjoyed it
very much indeed and in the course of the next few weeks
told it to so many people that Cor wished it had never
happened.

Then the King turned to Hwin and Bree and was just
as polite to them as to Aravis, and asked them a lot of
questions about their families and where they had lived in
Narnia before they had been captured. The Horses were
rather tongue-tied for they weren't yet used to being talked
to as equals by Humans – grown-up Humans, that is. They
didn't mind Aravis and Cor.

Presently Queen Lucy came out from the castle and
joined them and King Lune said to Aravis, 'My dear,
here is a loving friend of our house, and she has been seeing
that your apartments are put to rights for you better than
I could have done it.'

'You'd like to come and see them, wouldn't you?' said
Lucy, kissing Aravis. They liked each other at once and
soon went away together to talk about Aravis's bedroom
and Aravis's boudoir and about getting clothes for her,
and all the sort of things girls do talk about on such an
occasion.

After lunch, which they had on the terrace (it was cold
birds and cold game pie and wine and bread and cheese),
King Lune ruffled up his brow and heaved a sigh and said,
'Heigh-ho! We have still that sorry creature Rabadash on
our hands, my friends, and must needs resolve what to do
with him.'

Lucy was sitting on the King's right and Aravis on his
left. King Edmund sat at one end of the table and the Lord
Darrin faced him at the other. Dar and Peridan and Cor
and Corin were on the same side as the King.

'Your Majesty would have a perfect right to strike off his head,' said Peridan. 'Such an assault as he made puts him on a level with assassins.'

'It is very true,' said Edmund. 'But even a traitor may mend. I have known one that did.' And he looked very thoughtful.

'To kill this Rabadash would go near to raising war with the Tisroc,' said Darrin.

'A fig for the Tisroc,' said King Lune. 'His strength is in numbers and numbers will never cross the desert. But I have no stomach for killing men (even traitors) in cold blood. To have cut his throat in the battle would have eased my heart mightily: but this is a different thing.'

'By my counsel,' said Lucy, 'your Majesty shall give him another trial. Let him go free on strait promise of fair dealing in the future. It may be that he will keep his word.'

'Maybe Apes will grow honest, Sister,' said Edmund. 'But, by the Lion, if he breaks it again, it may be in such time and place that any of us could swap off his head in clean battle.'

'It shall be tried,' said the King: and then to one of the attendants, 'Send for the prisoner, friend.'

Rabadash was brought before them in chains. To look at him anyone would have supposed that he had passed the night in a noisome dungeon without food or water; but in reality he had been shut up in quite a comfortable room and provided with an excellent supper. But as he was sulking far too furiously to touch the supper and had spent the whole night stamping and roaring and cursing, he naturally did not now look his best.

'Your royal Highness needs not to be told,' said King

Lune, 'that by the law of nations as well as by all reasons of prudent policy, we have as good right to your head as ever one mortal man had against another. Nevertheless, in consideration of your youth and the ill nurture, devoid of all gentilesse and courtesy, which you have doubtless had in the land of slaves and tyrants, we are disposed to set you free, unharmed, on these conditions: first, that – '

'Curse you for a barbarian dog!' spluttered Rabadash. 'Do you think I will even hear your conditions? Faugh! You talk very largely of nurture and I know not what. It's easy, to a man in chains, ha! Take off these vile bonds, give me a sword, and let any of you who dares then debate with me.'

Nearly all the lords sprang to their feet, and Corin shouted:

'Father! Can I *box* him? Please.'

'Peace! Your Majesties! My Lords!' said King Lune. 'Have we no more gravity among us than to be so chafed by the taunt of a pajock? Sit down, Corin, or shalt leave the table. I ask your Highness again, to hear our conditions.'

'I hear no conditions from barbarians and sorcerers,' said Rabadash. 'Not one of you dare touch a hair of my head. Every insult you have heaped on me shall be paid with oceans of Narnian and Archenlandish blood. Terrible shall the vengeance of the Tisroc be: even now. But kill me, and the burnings and torturings in these northern lands shall become a tale to frighten the world a thousand years hence. Beware! Beware! Beware! The bolt of Tash falls from above!'

'Does it ever get caught on a hook half-way?' asked Corin.

'Shame, Corin,' said the King. 'Never taunt a man save when he is stronger than you: then, as you please.'

'Oh you foolish Rabadash,' sighed Lucy.

Next moment Cor wondered why everyone at the table had risen and was standing perfectly still. Of course he did the same himself. And then he saw the reason. Aslan was among them though no one had seen him coming. Rabadash started as the immense shape of the Lion paced softly in between him and his accusers.

'Rabadash,' said Aslan. 'Take heed. Your doom is very near, but you may still avoid it. Forget your pride (what have you to be proud of?) and your anger (who has done you wrong?) and accept the mercy of these good kings.'

Then Rabadash rolled his eyes and spread out his mouth into a horrible, long mirthless grin like a shark, and wagged his ears up and down (anyone can learn how to do this if they take the trouble). He had always found this very effective in Calormen. The bravest had trembled when he made these faces, and ordinary people had fallen to the floor, and sensitive people had often fainted. But what Rabadash hadn't realized is that it is very easy to frighten people who know you can have them boiled alive the moment you give the word. The grimaces didn't look at all alarming in Archenland; indeed Lucy only thought Rabadash was going to be sick.

'Demon! Demon! Demon!' shrieked the Prince. 'I know you. You are the foul fiend of Narnia. You are the enemy of the gods. Learn who *I* am, horrible phantasm. I am descended from Tash, the inexorable, the irresistible. The curse of Tash is upon you. Lightning in the shape of scorpions shall be rained on you. The mountains of Narnia shall be ground into dust. The –'

'Have a care, Rabadash,' said Aslan quietly. 'The doom is nearer now: it is at the door: it has lifted the latch.'

'Let the skies fall,' shrieked Rabadash. 'Let the earth gape! Let blood and fire obliterate the world! But be sure I will never desist till I have dragged to my palace by her hair the barbarian queen, the daughter of dogs, the –'

'The hour has struck,' said Aslan: and Rabadash saw, to his supreme horror, that everyone had begun to laugh.

They couldn't help it. Rabadash had been wagging his ears all the time and as soon as Aslan said, 'The hour has struck!' the ears began to change. They grew longer and more pointed and soon were covered with grey hair. And while everyone was wondering where they had seen ears like that before, Rabadash's face began to change too. It grew longer, and thicker at the top and larger eyed, and the nose sank back into the face (or else the face swelled out and became all nose) and there was hair all over it. And his arms grew longer and came down in front of him till his hands were resting on the ground: only they weren't hands, now, they were hoofs. And he was standing on all fours, and his clothes disappeared, and everyone laughed louder and louder (because they couldn't help it) for now what had been Rabadash was, simply and unmistakably, a donkey. The terrible thing was that his human speech lasted just a moment longer than his human shape, so that when he realized the change that was coming over him, he screamed out:

'Oh, not a Donkey! Mercy! If it were even a horse – even a horse – e'en – a –

hor – eeh – auh, eeh-auh.' And so the words died away
into a donkey's bray.

'Now hear me, Rabadash,' said Aslan. 'Justice shall
be mixed with mercy. You shall not always be an
Ass.'

At this of course the Donkey twitched its ears forward
– and that also was so funny that everybody laughed all the
more. They tried not to, but they tried in vain.

'You have appealed to Tash,' said Aslan. 'And in the
temple of Tash you shall be healed. You must stand before
the altar of Tash in Tashbaan at the great Autumn Feast
this year and there, in the sight of all Tashbaan, your ass's
shape will fall from you and all men will know you for
Prince Rabadash. But as long as you live, if ever you go
more than ten miles away from the great temple in Tashbaan you shall instantly become again as you now are.
And from that second change there will be no return.'

There was a short silence and then they all stirred and
looked at one another as if they were waking from sleep.
Aslan was gone. But there was a brightness in the air and
on the grass, and a joy in their hearts, which assured them
that he had been no dream: and anyway, there was the
donkey in front of them.

King Lune was the kindest-hearted of men and on seeing
his enemy in this regrettable condition he forgot all his
anger.

'Your royal Highness,' he said, 'I am most truly sorry
that things have come to this extremity. Your Highness
will bear witness that it was none of our doing. And of
course we shall be delighted to provide your Highness
with shipping back to Tashbaan for the – er – treatment
which Aslan has prescribed. You shall have every comfort

which your Highness's situation allows: the best of the cattle-boats – the freshest carrots and thistles – '

But a deafening bray from the Donkey and a well-aimed kick at one of the guards made it clear that these kindly offers were ungratefully received.

And here, to get him out of the way, I'd better finish off the story of Rabadash. He (or it) was duly sent back by boat to Tashbaan and brought into the temple of Tash at the great Autumn Festival, and then he became a man again. But of course four or five thousand people had seen the transformation and the affair could not possibly be hushed up. And after the old Tisroc's death when Rabadash became Tisroc in his place he turned out the most peaceable Tisroc Calormen had ever known. This was because, not daring to go more than ten miles from Tashbaan, he could never go on a war himself; and he didn't want his Tarkaans to win fame in the wars at his expense, for that is the way Tisrocs get overthrown. But though his reasons were selfish, it made things much more comfortable for all the smaller countries round Calormen. His own people never forgot that he had been a donkey. During his reign, and to his face, he was called Rabadash the Peacemaker, but after his death and behind his back he was called Rabadash the Ridiculous, and if you look him up in a good History of Calormen (try the local library) you will find him under that name. And to this day in Calormene schools, if you do anything unusually stupid, you are very likely to be called 'a second Rabadash'.

Meanwhile at Anvard everyone was very glad that he had been disposed of before the real fun began, which was a grand feast held that evening on the lawn before the castle, with dozens of lanterns to help the moonlight. And the wine flowed and tales were told and jokes were cracked, and then silence was made and the King's poet with two fiddlers stepped out into the middle of the circle. Aravis and Cor prepared themselves to be bored, for the only poetry they knew was the Calormene kind, and you know now what that was like. But at the very first scrape of the fiddles a rocket seemed to go up inside their heads, and the poet sang the great old lay of Fair Olvin and how he fought the Giant Pire and turned him into stone (and that is the origin of Mount Pire – it was a two-headed Giant) and won the Lady Liln for his bride; and when it was over they wished it was going to begin again. And though Bree couldn't sing he told the story of the fight at Zalindreh. And Lucy told again (they had all, except Aravis and Cor, heard it many times but they all wanted it again) the tale of the Wardrobe and how she and King Edmund and Queen Susan and Peter the High King had first come into Narnia.

And presently, as was certain to happen sooner or later, King Lune said it was time for young people to be in bed. 'And tomorrow, Cor,' he added, 'shalt come over all the castle with me and see the estres and mark all its strength and weakness: for it will be thine to guard when I'm gone.'

'But Corin will be the King then, Father,' said Cor.

'Nay, lad,' said King Lune, 'thou art my heir. The crown comes to thee.'

'But I don't want it,' said Cor. 'I'd far rather –'

''Tis no question what thou wantest, Cor, nor I either. 'Tis in course of law.'

'But if we're twins we must be the same age.'

'Nay,' said the King with a laugh. 'One must come first. Art Corin's elder by full twenty minutes. And his better too, let's hope, though that's no great mastery.' And he looked at Corin with a twinkle in his eyes.

'But, Father, couldn't you make whichever you like to be the next King?'

'No. The King's under the law, for it's the law makes him a king. Hast no more power to start away from thy crown than any sentry from his post.'

'Oh dear,' said Cor. 'I don't want to at all. And Corin – I am most dreadfully sorry. I never dreamed my turning up was going to chisel you out of your kingdom.'

'Hurrah! Hurrah!' said Corin. 'I shan't have to be King. I shan't have to be King. I'll always be a prince. It's princes have all the fun.'

'And that's truer than thy brother knows, Cor,' said King Lune. 'For this is what it means to be a king: to be first in every desperate attack and last in every desperate retreat, and when there's hunger in the land (as must be now and then in bad years) to wear finer clothes and laugh louder over a scantier meal than any man in your land.'

When the two boys were going upstairs to bed Cor again asked Corin if nothing could be done about it. And Corin said:

'If you say another word about it, I'll – I'll knock you down.'

It would be nice to end the story by saying that after that the two brothers never disagreed about anything again, but I am afraid it would not be true. In reality they quarrelled and fought just about as often as any other two boys would, and all their fights ended (if they didn't begin) with Cor getting knocked down. For though, when they had both grown up and become swordsmen, Cor was the more dangerous man in battle, neither he nor anyone else in the North Countries could ever equal Corin as a boxer. That was how he got his name of Corin Thunder-Fist; and how he performed his great exploit against the Lapsed Bear of Stormness, which was really a Talking Bear but had gone back to Wild Bear habits. Corin climbed up to its lair on the Narnian side of Stormness one winter day when the snow was on the hills and boxed it without a time-keeper for thirty-three rounds. And at the end it couldn't see out of its eyes and became a reformed character.

Aravis also had many quarrels (and, I'm afraid, even fights) with Cor, but they always made it up again: so that years later, when they were grown up, they were so used to quarrelling and making it up again that they got married so as to go on doing it more conveniently. And after King Lune's death they made a good King and Queen of Archenland and Ram the Great, the most famous of all the kings of Archenland, was their son. Bree and Hwin lived happily to a great age in Narnia and both got married but not to one another. And there weren't many months in which one or both of them didn't come trotting over the pass to visit their friends at Anvard.

If you have enjoyed this book and would like to know about others which we publish, why not join the Puffin Club? You will be sent the Club magazine *Puffin Post* four times a year and a smart badge and membership book. You will also be able to enter all the competitions. For details, send a stamped addressed envelope to:

The Puffin Club Dept A
Penguin Books Ltd
Harmondsworth
Middlesex